Death Chants

Also By Craig Kee Strete

DREAMS THAT BURN IN THE NIGHT

IF ALL ELSE FAILS . . .

Death Chants

Short Stories

CRAIG KEE STRETE

Doubleday
NEW YORK
1988

Library of Congress Cataloging-in-Publication Data
Strete, Craig.
Death chants.
1. Science fiction, American. 2. Indians of North
America—Fiction. I. Title.
PS3569.T6935D4 1988 813'.54 87-33143
ISBN 0-385-23353-1

Printed in the United States of America
First Edition

With love to dear dead Poek, whom I still love, and Timtim, who thinks I'm his mother, and to Irma, who made for me a home I never had and is truly the center of my universe

Contents

Death Chants

Introduction

HE IS AN AUTHOR OF THE UNRESPECTABLE.
HIS WRITING CONTAINS TWO GREAT LUSTS,
GENIUS AND EVIL.
IT IS HAUNTED
IT IS NIGHTMARE.
IT IS ANOTHER WORLD.
I CANNOT DESCRIBE IT SO WELL WITH WORDS
AS I COULD
WITH THE COLORS OF MADNESS AND THE HUES
OF OBSESSION.
THERE IS DALI IN THIS WRITER. HIS CANVASSES
ARE HERE,
STRETCHED BETWEEN THE PAGES OF THIS
STRANGE MAN'S BOOKS.
AS I READ, IN BENEATH THE DIFFICULTY OF
TRANSLATION, I
GET A SENSE OF ALIEN THOUGHT, OF
AUTOMATISM IN A
FRIGHTENING SENSATION, AS IF NO MIND HAD
PUT THESE WORDS
ON PAPER, AS IF INSTEAD, IT HAD COME, FULLY
ARMED, BY
SPONTANEOUS COMBUSTION.

IT IS THE KIND OF WRITING THAT IS
WONDERFUL AT NIGHT.
IT IS BETRAYAL. IT IS RARE AND TERRIBLE AND
DROLL.
IT ENGAGES THE EYE AS IT EVISCERATES IT.
TO HEAR IT READ IS TO BE SPLASHED WITH AN
UNKNOWN BLOOD.

I CELEBRATE THIS UNNOBLE SAVAGE WHOSE
WRITING TELLS ME
THAT NIGHTMARE IS REALISM.
I CELEBRATE IT.
DESPITE MEETING HIM FACE TO FACE, I REFUSE
TO BELIEVE
THESE ARE THE WORKS OF A YOUNG MAN.
THEY ARE TOO MUCH LIKE THE MEMOIRS OF AN
OLD MAN WHO
REMEMBERS THE HORRORS OF LIFE AND FEELS
THE METAL TEETH
OF DECAY EATING AT HIS SKIN.
LIKE A NEW DREAM, HIS WRITING SEIZES THE
MIND.
THE WRITINGS OF THIS YOUNG MAN ARE
ÉCART ABSOLOU.

BARCELONA, SPAIN
SALVADOR DALI

Lives Far Child

"It was the beatings," was all Lives Far would say, and she knelt down by the bed with the red and blue Navaho blanket and wept.

"Seems to me, you married a hard one," said Navana, her father. He sat cross-legged by the door of the hogan. His hands were busy carving a small whistle out of elk bone.

"I don't mind the beatings so much," said Lives Far, "but it is not good for my children to see. It shows them the wrong path in life."

Navana watched her with vague unease. Lives Far was five years old, just five, but she was a strange, strange child.

Navana blew the bone scrapings off the whistle and put it to his lips. He blew gently on it and it made a pleasing birdlike trill.

Lives Far turned and looked in his direction, her eyes brightening in spite of the tears.

He held it out to her. "I made this for you, little one."

She came toward him eagerly and took it from his hands. Her face was still wet with tears.

"Make it sing, Lives Far," said Navana and his face lit with a brief hope.

She started to put it to her lips, delight in her eyes, but something stopped the delight and she became solemn and her hands closed in a fist over the whistle.

"I'll keep it and give it to my children," she said. "They are waiting for me outside."

Navana's second wife, Winter Gatherer, stood in the doorway. She was of another tribe and her ways were sometimes hard.

"That child must be punished!" she said bitterly. "We have heard enough of her lies."

Navana put his hand over the small child fist that held the elk bone whistle.

He smiled down at the child with sadness in his eyes.

"My people teach that lies are blackhearted and a child would be beaten if it talked like . . ." Winter Gatherer started again.

Navana turned on her angrily.

"I have heard enough about your people and your ways! We do not beat our little ones! Always gentleness, always respect and understanding, so I have been raised and so I will raise my children! Our way is better."

"A stupid way to raise children," she said. "But something will have to be done about her, if you're too cowardly to beat her."

"Go outside and play," Navana told the child.

"Yes. I've got washing to do and corn to weed and hoe," said Lives Far. "And I better see to fixing supper for Thomas or he'll beat me again."

She went outside, moving slowly, like an old woman bent under the burdens of a lifetime.

At birth, Lives Far was a child unlike other children. Her mother, Navana's first wife, slowly bleeding to death under the birth blankets, had looked into the tiny red face and feared greatly what she saw. Her own death, red and inevitable beneath the Pendleton blanket, did not scare her.

Death was an old friend but the things she saw in her child's eyes were older than anything that ever moved in her world.

When Navana had come at last into the quickening room, he saw the obscene birds of birth and death perched on the same withered branch of his living tree. His wife took his face in her hands when he bent down over her. Gently she turned him away so that he might not look upon the face of the child at her breast. For children at birth cannot hide themselves from the world until life is strong in their bodies.

And she feared that seeing the child for what it might be, he might wish to destroy it.

"I call this child, Lives Far," she said speaking prophecy, and she kept Navana busy with her own death until the child had taken enough of the world's wind into its body, enough living strength to hide its true self. The old ones say such a happening is an evil birth, evil when the greedy child sucks the life out of its own mother. But the child came into the world, evil or not, and was loved and grew under Navana's nurturing wing.

Navana knew Lives Far never played as other children played. She just sat in the sun and talked to people who were not there.

Lives Far, so she said, was married to a white man and had two children by him. His name was Thomas Morgan and he drank and beat her and was evil. Yes, that was what she said. And she described him in great detail, in a way no child of five could possibly know.

"Thomas burns with drink and it burns his head inside, burns someplace deep until his hair no longer feels like hair, but like a scalp of ashes.

"Poor Thomas," she said and her child's voice seemed to forgive him everything. "The drink burns his tongue in the roof of his mouth so the words of his war nightmares can't escape as he sleeps. It started not just with his liking it, but his needing it, the drink, always the drink, because it is the water of war and it made one forget to be afraid and promised other kinds of forgetfulness."

Navana had felt like screaming in the face of such solemn, straight-faced gibberish, if a part of him had not been a little shocked by it, and a little frightened of it as well.

For though Navana did not heed the words of the old ones, who would have seen this child, Lives Far, who took her own mother out of this world, destroyed as an evil thing, still Navana was disturbed and uneasy sometimes when the child was acting this way. He loved her with all his heart but his mind sometimes saw shadows lurking all about her, and a darkness he could not fathom.

"But the forgetfulness must have been too deep or not deep enough. The Thomas Morgan that I married never came back from the war."

Her face was full of sorrow. "He doesn't sleep with me anymore," she confided in a childish whisper. "I've begged him, pleaded with him, but he won't touch me now. He just drinks now and sometimes beats me and always, always, has nightmares. He used to be so sweet when he made love to me. Now he's a stranger to my bed."

Coming from the lips of a five-year-old, it was a tiny, almost mad horror.

Navana brushed the elk bone shavings off his lap.

Winter Gatherer remained in the doorway, looking out at the squash garden. Her beauty was like a weapon, her sharp tongue the point of her spear.

"She's just sitting there like always, Navana, talking to her invisible family. She's head-sick," said Winter Gatherer, fingering a beaded choker around her neck.

"She was always a big-eyed child. Always in a dream," remembered Navana. "The sky is full of rabbits, yellow and brown ones, she would tell me. Or fish are swimming in my ears, Father, make them stop."

"Childish dreams are one thing," said Winter Gatherer. "But these strange dreams have grown to truth in her mind. She is like one possessed."

"Many were the strange dreams I myself had as a child, but as time moved me down the path of life, those dreams left me and new and proper ones came to take their place. So it will be with her, if we give her time," said Navana, but there was very little hope in his voice as much as he wanted to believe it.

Lives Far screamed.

Navana and Winter Gatherer ran outside.

They expected danger but saw none.

Just Lives Far alone, her eyes red with weeping, sprawled in a heap in the dust.

"What's wrong, little one? Spider bite you? See a snake?" asked Navana with loving concern, suddenly conscious of clenched fists and relaxing them.

"He's dead," she said.

"Who's dead?" said Winter Gatherer suspiciously, her eyes flashing darkly.

"My husband, Thomas," said Lives Far. "Mostly it's the drink I blame. It's what caused most of our trouble too. I always said it would be the death of him. And now it's taken him away forever. But he wouldn't listen to me. He just wouldn't listen, so he got into a fight in a bar and another white man stabbed him. Left me and the children all alone."

Navana wiped his face with his hand, anxiety plain in his face.

"Now I have to ask you if we can go bring the children to stay with us. It isn't right that the children should be home alone when I work. I know I'll have to work. Thomas fed us at least, but with him gone, it'll be up to me," said Lives Far solemnly, regarding each of them gravely.

"I'm sorry to hear he's dead," said Navana, not sure if he liked this sudden turn of events. If this meant an end to her strange make-believe and a return to being his little five-year-old girl, then Navana was all for it. But he had little real hope.

"We have to go get the children," insisted Lives Far.

"You don't have a husband and you don't have any damn children!" said Winter Gatherer, arms thrust out angrily at her side. She was like an angry snake, coiled to strike.

Navana looked at his wife, shaking his head no. "I'll handle this."

He bent down and put his arm around the frail child. He gently wiped the tears from her eyes.

"Listen to me, Lives Far. If we go to find your children, and there are no children, no Thomas, dead or otherwise, will you put aside this dream once and for all?"

"What dream?" asked Lives Far. "Please, Father, they are blood of your blood. You have to go with me to pick them up."

Navana decided to take the challenge.

"All right, little one, do you know the road to take?"

"West," said Lives Far. "Until we reach the great rock shaped like a turtle, there we turn left and then follow the stream bed. That's where they buried Thomas this morning. And my children will be just down the road from there."

Navana stood up, looked to the west and then nodded once, having come to a decision.

"Then west we shall go."

"Leave me out of the we," said Winter Gatherer. "I'm sick of the whole business."

Navana looked at her for a moment as if seeing her for the first time, and not exactly liking what he saw.

"No need for you to come," said Navana. "I'll saddle up just the one horse for me and Lives Far."

"Eat supper first. Man's going to be a damn fool, he ought to at least have a full belly first."

"I've got a full belly of something already," he said and he took Lives Far by the hand and led her to the barn.

While they were saddling up the horse, they heard the back door of the house slam.

"Isn't Winter Gatherer coming to see her grandchildren?" asked Lives Far.

"No," said Navana grimly, tightening the cinch strap under the belly of the horse. "I figure she's heading into the trading post. Probably to visit a couple relatives of hers that live in bottles. We don't need her anyway."

"How far do you reckon this place is?" said Navana, leading the horse out of the barn.

Lives Far trotted along at his side. "Years and years in Indian time," said Lives Far. "It's not far at all."

Navana swung up easily into the saddle. He bent down, reached for the child and swung her up gracefully behind him on the horse.

They trotted down the long dusty road to the west. The sun walked across the sky. The air was as dry as dust under a dead snake and the heat rose off the road in waves. Sweat soaked them both and they swayed dizzily in the saddle with the heat.

As the afternoon moved toward evening, Navana noticed that Lives Far was blood-red with the sun and the heat. She was barely conscious, her arms, loosening moment by moment around his waist.

"I've been down this road a thousand times, little one, as far west as it goes and I've never seen a rock shaped like a turtle."

With an effort the child opened her eyes, and moved her head so that she could see past him.

"There!" she cried. "There it is! Just like I said."

Navana turned and his eyes widened in horror.

A landslide had dumped a pile of rocks across one side of the road as it entered Devil's Canyon. Seen from a distance, the tumbled heap of stones did indeed look very much like a turtle.

"Funny nobody ever told me about that landslide," said Navana, shaking his head in bewilderment. "I was through here just last week and there was nothing like this."

"This is where we turn," said Lives Far. "Hurry, Father. We're almost there."

Reluctantly, with no sense of the make-believe coming to an end, Navana turned the horse and they moved on.

The horse almost stumbled as it moved down into the bed of a long-dry stream.

"Now just follow the stream bed and we'll be there soon," said Lives Far. "I can't wait to see my children!"

Heartsick and feeling a growing uneasiness, Navana let the horse follow the stream bed at a walk.

The light of day was beginning to fade. The long shadows of night began marching across the sky. Now the stream bed seemed to melt under their feet and the sky was vanishing into darkness.

"Child, in all my years, I don't recall a stream being here. It's near dark and getting hard to see the way. We ought to be home. Maybe we better turn back now."

"But we're almost there," cried Lives Far. "See over there, that's the graveyard!"

She was pointing off to the right.

Navana turned in horror and saw a small area of ground, fenced off with wrought iron. It was the kind of fence the white men used around their burying places. Navana felt raw pulsing terror rising in him.

Lives Far let go of his waist and slid off the horse. She hit hard, overbalanced and fell forward on her face. She bounced to her feet, ignoring her injuries, and began running toward the graveyard.

"Thomas!" she cried.

"Wait!" screamed Navana. "Come back!"

Lives Far ran through the front gate and dashed through the rows of tombstones, thrusting up into the night like the pale white stone fingers of dead men.

Navana jumped down off the horse and ran after her, screaming for her to stop.

She was lost to sight from him somewhere in the cold gray rows of stone.

He stumbled through the growing dark, calling out her name.

He couldn't find her anywhere.

His terror and panic grew. Each step seemed to take him deeper into darkness. He passed by a group of small tombstones at the far end of the graveyard and then he heard her voice.

"Poor Thomas. I loved you once." That was Lives Far's voice coming eerily from somewhere off to the right.

He staggered toward her.

"Lives Far!" he screamed.

A cloud passed overhead and the new moon cast a gray light on the graveyard.

In the distance he thought he saw her hunched over a small tombstone, her back to him.

"Lives Far, come away from there! You are disturbing the dead and doing them a dishonor! None of our people are buried here. Come away, child. I know you are sick in your mind. Very sick, Lives Far, and I am going to take you home now!"

Resolutely, he moved toward her, past the ice palaces of cold speechless stone.

"Don't you want to pay your respects to Thomas, Father?"

He came and stood over her, like a sad shadow in the moonlight.

"My poor little one," he said and he bent down to take her in his arms. But as he stooped over, the moon plainly illuminated the lettering on the gravestone.

HERE LIES THOMAS MORGAN
BELOVED HUSBAND OF LIVES FAR MORGAN
1830–1873

Navana backed away in terror.

"Where am I? Where is this place?"

"Father," said Lives Far. "We have to go now. My children are just down the way."

"No, child," said Navana, his voice high with fear. "We must go back the way we came!"

"But I don't want to go back," said Lives Far. "I don't want to be a child back there. I belong here."

"Where is here?" asked Navana.

"Why, 1873 of course," said Lives Far. "The year I lost my husband, Thomas."

"We have to go back!" he cried, terror etching the lines of his face. He turned and looked at the lettering on the gravestone. He knew that the date had to be right, but it could not be! When he had gotten up that morning, it was as the white men had numbered it, 1845, not 1873!

"I can't leave my children," said Lives Far. "You can't make me go back! I won't go! You're dead anyway now."

Lives Far started to back away from him.

"Wait! Listen to me!" he cried but she turned and began to run from him. "Go back!" she said. "You're dead here. And my children need me."

Navana wanted to run after her but terror held him like a dark mother embracing a night child.

She seemed to grow as she ran away from him. Gone were the short little legs of a child, coltish and awkward. Now she ran with the grace of a young girl, as if now seeking the first ground-devouring strides of womanhood.

And then as she passed finally into the distance, she seemed to run with the full-legged gait of a woman.

"LIVES FAR!" His anguished cry chased her all through the moonlit night.

The child was gone.

As much as he wanted to run after her, a certainty as black as night itself, held him back.

He knew that on the other side of that graveyard, somewhere in 1873, his child was a woman grown with children of her own and he was a tree of nothing but bones, shaking no more wind in its white branches.

Navana stood there like a lost deer in the night wind.

He looked back the way he had come and thought now of the childless house back there waiting for him, the empty maternal rooms, the dust gathering on soon-to-be-forgotten toys.

Could a life be lived in that house now? His thoughts turned unhappily to Winter Gatherer and to the rest of their journey of days together.

What did he have to go back to, with Lives Far gone from him?

A man without children was no better than a wind in the grave.

He squared his shoulders and began to walk in the direction Lives Far had gone. If the living can see the dead, then the dead can see the living, this was in his mind.

He stepped outside the back gate of the cemetery and his feet began to sink into the ground.

So this is what death is like, he thought.

Then he made a great effort to straighten his shoulders once more and again walk in the direction Lives Far had gone. With each step, he sank deeper as the dark earth reached up to pull the white bones down through his skin. His skin seemed to run away like water into the thirsty earth, seeking its own level.

He did not die as he left the cemetery. He could not die.

In Lives Far Woman's world, for five cold long years, he had already been dead.

In the Belly of the Death Mother

The sun burned in the reservation sky like a fever dream animal. The old woman stood outside the house and looked out over the dead land, staring at nothing. There was no feeling in her, no pain or hope or even a sense of loss.

That morning she had seen how things were in the darkened room and she was not sorry.

Even now, as she waited for him to die, to sing his death song, the shadows that had walked through all her days made her still and quiet within herself.

A lone hawk wheeled above her, screaming in the sky.

She stared up at it, seeing its deadly wings slashing across the blue sky like angry knives.

From inside the building, that crumbling stone and brick ruin that had contained the larger part of their life together and now held their end, all was quiet. Almost too quiet.

She strained to hear, as if listening for something that might stalk her, that might come for her. She heard only distant bird noises and the hot dull sound of insects at first and then, faintly, the murmur of a voice.

His voice. Chanting perhaps. Speaking once again to the ancestors, perhaps telling them he was now ready to journey among them.

She would have been content to wait outside until it was over. Maybe the old man wanted it that way. It was hard to tell. They did not talk to each other much. The hurts of the past had grown like a stone canyon between them.

The sun beat down mercilessly on her head and back, but she was used to it. The sun was inescapable, and unrelenting, like life on the reservation.

The sound of his voice, echoing inside the dark building, changed.

Now it sounded like the old man was crying.

It was not what she would have expected.

She opened the badly hung door and stared into the evil-smelling gloom. She saw his crooked back, broke saddled with his old age, distorted in the ugly shadow.

There was a strangeness in the room, in the air itself, as if something had come crawling out of a grave and passed through the old stone and brick walls of the house. She shuddered. It was cold in here, impossibly cold for a day as hot as this.

There was a smell in here, an alien scent, not death, for that smell was all too familiar on the reservation, but of something else. Perhaps the life's breath of some night walker.

What had happened in here, she could not know. Nor did she care to know. The old man had his shaman's secrets and she never trespassed on them, for they were evil secrets.

"What's wrong?" she asked. "Why do you cry?"

"I cry because I touched the faces of the dead. I felt their cold lips brush against mine," said the old man. He said it, but it was not true, not completely true. He could not cry. He had seen too much in and out of life for tears.

But he could never tell her this. His fear, always about her, about all the men and women he knew, was that too much of his real self, changed forever by the strange life beyond life he had met and paid worship to, would someday show and they would think him no longer human.

"You should take the medicine," said the old woman, staring at the untouched bowl at his feet.

"I'll take it when my bones are two days dead and piercing mother earth, seeking cool water."

"It is late in the day and you are tired," she said.

"It is early in the first morning and I, just born, shall go dancing in a warm grave in the belly of the death mother." The old man bared his yellow teeth in a cruel smile.

"I think not," she said and recalled something that was long past. Everything was old and dying and long past in her world.

"The sun reaches across the sky, burning the day left to me," said the old man. "I have seen the last of it. I shall see it walk the sky no more. I've had a vision and the land of dark beckons me, old woman."

He lifted his hand and stared at it. "I can see the bones showing through." He seemed suddenly pleased by that. There was a strange, terrible smile on his face.

She felt her face growing cold, her own heart going distant like a star in an unfriendly sky. He was a stranger to her, as he had always been and would be. She felt nothing for him, only small sorrow for herself. Her life had been empty, with no blood on her knife and no children to crawl across the cold years with their welcome gift of sudden and lasting warmth.

He had taken her youth from her, stripped it from her long ago, and the memory of it did not sleep easily, if it slept at all.

"You are too eager for death, old man!" she accused him. "Has it ever been the way of our people to embrace death? To welcome it as an old friend, yes, that is our way, but you, old man, in your terrible way, you almost make of death, an old lover come to make you feel young again."

"Yes. Death is a sweet, ice-skinned woman, who kisses and kills in a darkened room. I long for her touch. I welcome the growing cold, the cool hiss of it. Yes. I desire it greatly."

"You wish to be rid of me, rid of this life."

"Yes." The old man admitted it, not knowing if the words hurt and not caring.

Years gone by, the words would have stung like hail on bare skin, but she was past all that.

"You are a ghost, a shadow even now, old man, but you have long been dead with the wanting of it." The old woman stared at the room, seeing the great emptiness. "We should have had children. We could have chosen life over your magics, your strange journeys into . . ."

"Be still! I have no regrets! I have lived as I willed it," said the old man, turning his one good eye away from her. "Now is not the time to change the path, old woman. That time is past. You could have had a different life but you walked my road, so let that be an end to moaning about it."

"Why have you always pursued me with your coldness, given deadening chase to the heart of me? Why always to me, I who have wished only to live with you and love you?"

"Power was more to me than you. Power I could not always have. But you I always had."

"You were born with the dead. You are a grave shadow, but yet with my old heart in your hand, I, now old and gray and used up, I am the loving one you murdered."

He turned his one good eye toward her and was shocked by what he saw. The bird of death, long and black and eyeless, hovered above her and sand seemed to pour from the empty sockets of her hair-covered skull.

The illusion passed but not the reason for it.

"You!" said the old man. He shook his head at the wonder of it. "As I die, so do you! I, who see many things no one else can see, did not know it."

"I felt the little knife of death in my chest this morning and knew the sun would not see me again," she said and the look on her face was almost apologetic. "I have packed my face for the journey to take my name out of the world."

The old man seemed to shrink back inside himself. This was not something he had counted on. New thoughts, unwanted, sprang to his mind. Feelings he hated within himself arose and overcame him.

Suddenly, he regretted everything he had ever done to her.

For a moment he wanted to ask her forgiveness. There would be a rightness to that act. But he could not bring himself to do this thing because his heart walked on the ground.

His whole life was based on mastery, over her, over the world of shadows and men. If she saw the tender heart, his true sorrow, she would gain mastery over him, and that he could never allow.

He was a man with many dark secets, but the darkest, most unspeakable secret of all, was an old love for her, a love unspoken and buried like a war pipe in the grave of yesterday.

As he thought of her, a thousand thousand remembered cruelties assaulted him, each memory like another bitter branch on his funeral pyre.

Not forgiveness, no, that was not in him for the asking, but sorrow, that at least he could admit to.

"Yes, old woman," he said, shutting his good eye, the words coming slowly, painfully, "I've treated you badly."

"It doesn't matter," she said and he knew she did not mean it.

He thought of all the women he'd had, the boasts he had made to her about it, reveling in his own proud male blindness.

Most of the stories had been lies. But she had believed him and been hurt, again and again.

When the power eluded him, when the tantalizing magics danced just beyond his grasp, then and only then did he find solace in his women. But even then, he talked more conquests than he had made, that was his way. Lie or truth, the hurt was the same.

"You know all my old evils and cruelties. And there were many of them. I cannot unmake them nor can I forget them. These old wounds are too much with me now. I find them large now in my heart," he said.

"Don't talk about them," she said.

"I had my outside women and . . ."

"Yes," she said. "There were women to share the warmth you could not give me. But why talk of it? That warmth has long since cooled, the fires are dead, and the arms that held you do not have you as I now have you."

"I traveled in distant worlds. It was something you could not understand. I walked with the night walkers, danced under strange suns, tasted poisoned burning water from hidden rivers no man ever saw. I turned on the spit of my ribs in fires from other suns. Swam like an insect drowning in the nightpool oceans of other worlds. You could not know the gleaming night horrors I have seen, met and embraced, sometimes held in my arms, and even put my lips to and drank, inhaling the dark foul rich blood. Such glory and strangeness did I have. But I could not take you with me. That at least you understood. You stayed in your own world and you were safe there. You were just a woman who had never traveled."

"And so you needed the taste and touch of other dark women with eyes like black jewels who would understand your strangeness in ways that I could not. I have heard the tale often, but does it ever excuse the old hurts?" she said, but there was no tone of accusation in her voice, only acceptance.

"Yes," said the old man. "Strange and beautiful women who ran with me to the far places, women without human names, and I found solace and some little comfort in their shared heat from the spirit storms I journeyed in. So it was."

The old woman folded her hands in her lap. "You knew a

pretty woman when you saw one. There was one called Nihali. You talked of her often. You loved this one much."

The old man's eyes clouded with sudden memory. "Yes, that one. It was in the heat of a now dead summer. She was a night child, half woman, half darkness. I burned in terrible fire for that one. But she is gone as they are all gone and I am here with you. So it is."

The old woman bowed her head.

"I still remember the hurt, old man."

His eyes flashed with anger, anger more at himself than at her. "You cried that season more than ever. You waited up for me late in the night. Your heart smiled when I came back to you but your eyes said something else. I always knew the feelings that lived in your eyes. They were truer than the heart, which is often a great pretender."

"I tried to understand," she said, not looking at him.

"But failed, as you must, being only a simple living woman of one world. For what did you know of my great medicine? I was a Great Spirit Being and drank of things that other men could not taste."

"There was a time when I wanted to scratch her eyes out or drown myself in the river. That feeling is as dead as my youth. I told myself that what you did was nothing bad-hearted. That all men did it. It was a lie because few men love night spirits, but it comforted me, that old lie. In time, old man, I think I even forgot it was a lie."

The old man felt the bones of his chest. "My time comes soon, old woman. I dwell in sorrowful ways upon the old hurts, but I was what I am and will always be."

"This is not a time to ask forgiveness, nor can you speak for that because it is not your way. It is all long forgotten. You were good to me in your fashion and we had a life together. Out of strangeness we wove it, and nothing else matters," she said.

"It is not for you to forgive me anyway. I must forgive myself if that is what must be. Only I know what I have done. I have lain with the dark and terrible ones." There was still an element of boasting in his speech for the old habit died hard. "The scars of that must survive in me always." Something passed like a shadow across his face and for an instant he looked haunted, tormented by all the old treacheries. His eyes were dark and uncertain.

And then it happened. The old woman saw into his power and into the distance beyond it, to the end and the overcoming of him, once and for all time. She had never felt revenge in the snake of her old woman's heart, but now it leaped with fangs from her breast.

"You know me and you do not know me. I had my guilty secrets, too," she said proudly, the lie coming uneasily to her tongue. A lie was new to her, alien to her being.

The old man smiled, not believing her. He felt pain in his chest, but the thought that she could possibly have had a secret sin still made him smile.

"Keep your secrets, old woman. You might scare me with them and the shock would kill me." He almost laughed at that.

His mockery reached her not at all.

"I must tell you about it. I don't want you to feel so guilty, thinking you are the only one who has gone down strange roads. It will ease your heart to hear it. I never had the courage to tell you before."

He was contemptuous. "Nayee! You never had the courage to . . ."

But she interrupted him. "I slept with a bonepicker. With the night guardian who dances the bone dance in the sacred burying grounds of our people."

"You didn't do it." He waved his hands, as though shaking something away, but his voice was broken like a traveling wind.

"But I did." The old woman held on to the lie, sensing its power. "A long long time ago. And why shouldn't I? Is the world of spirits for men only? A woman can live at night as well as a man."

"NO! NO! It cannot be!" said the old man.

"It was a night when you were with some other woman, witch, or humankind, I did not know or care, and I was alone. It was a time of season change when the whole world is restless. Not like now, not like the burnt ashes of unchanging summer. It was night, and the stars seemed to fall in my hair and the windows were open to the wind and sky and he who waited for me . . ."

"When?" raged the old man, not believing but yet . . . "When?"

"It seems like only a few nights ago. Like last night and every night. I heard the birds dancing night love in the trees. I saw people passing on the distant road and every voice and sound, birds and unknown travelers, seemed to whisper, 'Why are you alone?' "

"You lie!" insisted the old man.

"I felt that if I stayed a moment longer by myself my heart would tear itself out of my breast. I put on my best dress, the one trimmed with porcupine quill and elk teeth. I wore my white buckskin leggings. Yes, and I went into the night and sought him out."

"No one would touch you!" screamed the old man. "Who would dare my wrath, my great killing powers!"

"Yes." And now she had to smile at her own cleverness. "Your power was great and all men feared you. All living men. But the dead fear nothing."

"Who? Who was it?" he demanded to know.

"The night walker. The nameless one," she said. "He was young and old and ugly and handsome. He was all things and nothing. And he was strong and quick in the dark and he waited for me."

"LIES!"

"He undressed me beneath the burial rack of my father's father. His hands were like ice on a frozen man's dead face, but they burned me just the same." The old woman untied her long braid, slowly unknotting the one long clump of gray hair. Carefully, like a young girl who flirted, she did not look at him.

"He never spoke but he caught hold of me in the dark and, in his strange embrace, I forgot you."

"You are lying," he said, as if trying to convince himself. "You made it all up."

Slowly he rose to his feet. He stood in front of her. She saw his wrinkled face and his white hair and the look in his eyes. He looked like a traveler from a far place, like someone she did not want to meet.

"He would not have had you," insisted the old man. "I know

their ways and you had nothing he would have wanted, not power, not beauty."

"Oh, but he did." She watched his face now and the desire burned in her to put her mark upon him and she felt a sudden strength. "But I did not know that you cared. Now you must know how I felt each night you were gone."

In the telling, it became real even to her, this imaginary night of long ago.

"I still say you lie." But he was uncertain. "And even if you found him, even if you had night-seeing eyes to see the spirit being, he wouldn't have wanted you! They have eyes only for great power or great beauty."

"But I was beautiful that night," she said.

"You were always ugly," he insisted, in his old unkind way.

"To you, perhaps," said the old woman. "But I knew how to make myself pretty for him. His eyes and hands told me a thousand times that I was beautiful."

"You are out of your mind. Approaching death, that terrible bird I see on your shoulder, hungry and shriveled, has driven you crazy," said the old man, casting about for something, for some kind of explanation, for it was never her way to lie. Never. He considered this, wanting to convince himself that what he had said was true before he believed her completely, but there was no madness in her manner or speech. The old man shuddered as if something had passed by, casting a dark shadow over him.

"You were drunk. You dreamed it. It did not happen, you only think it happened," he said.

She shook her head. "One night, if it had only been one night, then yes, I could have been drunk. One night even that I could have dreamed. But it was many nights, a hundred, a thousand, how many I do not know, for we were both hungry in the dark. Like that, drunk or dreaming, it is only possible that it happened."

And then for the first time in a life without tears, the old man wept.

She was silent, not looking at him.

He felt something breaking inside himself, shattering into

anguished fragments. Dreams rose and died and memories of nights long ago were like spears through his heart.

In a few words, a lifetime of mastery, of dancing unaffected above the shallow things of everyone else's life, was shattered. Like an eagle with an arrow through its wings, he fell from the sky, and her earth, which had never been his, came rushing up to meet him.

Now he did not know who he was anymore.

She said nothing, continued only to not look at him. He touched her arm with one trembling hand but she seemed not to notice.

"What are you thinking about? Do you hear what I say? Answer me!" he cried, because for the first time he felt he did not know what was in her mind. "What are you thinking about?"

"About him," she said, and the lie was bigger and easier on her tongue. "And I shall think of him until the end. He was all I had."

The old man reeled back as if struck.

"You make it up. You want to frighten me!"

"Why should I frighten you? You have seen too many dark things to take fright at anything an old woman could say." Her voice was serene, unconcerned. "We both did what we wanted to do."

"You were mine! Mine!" said the old man and the tears fell with each word.

"Once . . . but not only yours," she said.

Death came into the old man, creeping outward from the heart. He had time for only a few words.

"You've ruined me."

He slipped to the floor, no longer able to stand up.

"Now I am afraid of death! Afraid! Always I thought I understood the living. That I saw into their hearts and knew all that was to be known. But now, I know I have never known you, never known the secrets of your heart! I never had mastery over you. Never! Never mastery over you who I thought to be life itself. And now I am ruined. Ruined! For if I could not conquer life, then death will certainly destroy me!"

He looked up into her eyes and saw the answer.

"Yes," she said, and it was the most terrible word he had ever heard in his life, and it was the last word.

She watched in the comfortable dark, waiting to die beside him as soon she must, and felt young, almost reborn. She was like a woman newly in love, in that first all-consuming love that is sweetest of all.

He was hers now. He died belonging to her and to no one else, not to himself, or to the spirits of the far country.

She waited for death happily now, for the heart of woman is only happy when it owns all it has conquered.

And her magic had been so strong that she had conquered the world.

Another Horse of a Different Technicolor

Two old men sat side by side in rocking chairs like two tame birds perched on the lid of a coffin.

One was white, the other was Indian.

John Forbes had a beard.

He was the white one.

He coughed a lot, dressed forty years behind the fashions and chain-smoked cigarettes with slot-machine motions.

Red Horse was in the other chair. He was dressed in old jeans, a bright blue shirt good enough to steal and a pair of old cowboy boots even a dead man wouldn't want to wear.

He had an old corncob pipe stuck in his mouth and his thick gray hair was tied none too neatly in braids.

Jack Forbes inhaled deeply on his cigarette and coughed so hard he blew cigarette ashes all over his shirt. Despite the years that had marked his face, there was still a great deal of strength to be seen there. He had the air about him of a man who had met life headlong and unflinchingly. He had the look of a man accustomed to being in command.

Red Horse noticed the cough. "Man your age, ought to have learned how to smoke by now."

Jack Forbes stopped coughing and looked over at Red Horse. He wiped the back of his hand across his mouth before he spoke.

"I made you a star. You should be happy."

"I wanted to be a planet," said the old Indian calmly.

"You can pretend against it but you had it all. My films made you larger than life."

Red Horse lit his pipe, puffed on it contentedly.

"I was not larger than life, just thicker above the neck," said Red Horse. "I made faces for a living. You call it acting. Running twenty miles a day in front of a camera to hit somebody over the head with a rubber tomahawk is not a serious way to go through life."

"There you go, poor-mouthing everything. You're just angry at me because you couldn't handle the success," said Forbes.

Red Horse shrugged. "I didn't know I had any. After all, I was in your movies."

"You had your name up in lights. If that's not success, I don't know what is."

"You're right. You don't know what is. The kind of success you are talking about tastes like your foot feels when it falls asleep. It is crawling on your hands and knees at two hundred miles an hour."

"You had success," insisted John Forbes. "You just were too Indian to capitalize on it. I see you haven't changed.

"You can say what you want about being in my films but I filmed what I knew. I don't regret it. In the old West, men were men."

"And they smelled like horses," added Red Horse, trying to be accurate.

Forbes stared off into the distance, seeing something unseen. "Remember the first film I directed you in?"

Forbes smiled at the memory, turning to look at Red Horse. "*Return of the Apache Devil.* It was a two-reeler made for the old Republic studios. Made the whole damn thing in three days. It made money hand over fist."

"How could I remember that far back? When you've fallen off one horse, you've fallen off them all," said Red Horse.

Forbes went on, "Republic thought I was a genius. Two reels in three days and a first-time director to boot. Hell, if they'd only known. I was in Mexico two days before and DRANK the water!" He tugged uncomfortably at his pants. "I went fast because I HAD to go fast. I had the one-shot trots. Should have bottled that stuff and sold it to producers with directors behind schedule."

Red Horse nodded. "We shot more film when you were on the toilet. That's why we finished the film so damn quick."

Forbes was indignant. "That's a goddamn lie!"

Red Horse remained calm. "Indians never tell lies. They just don't tell the truth."

Forbes tapped his chest with his finger.

"I directed ever' damn foot of that film."

"Same method in toilet. When you find something that works, I say use it every chance you get."

Forbes scowled at Red Horse and then bent over and opened a paper bag at his feet. Red Horse watched with obvious interest as Forbes took out two cans of beer. Forbes glanced at Red Horse to see if he wanted one. Red Horse nodded yes with evident eagerness and Forbes opened both cans.

Red Horse started to reach for the beer but a thought suddenly occurred to Forbes and he just missed handing the can of beer to Red Horse. Forbes took an absentminded sip out of the can of beer meant for Red Horse.

"Tell me, Red Horse, why did you ever come to Hollywood in the first place?"

Red Horse stared at the can of beer with fascination as he answered. "I was dreaming. I hoped to penetrate a house of knowledge which I believed lay beneath the sea. When I returned to the land of men, I wanted the spirits of this great knowledge to make my people walk in beauty."

Forbes was incredulous. "You came to Hollywood for that?"

Red Horse shrugged, withdrawing the hand that had reached out for the beer. "Well actually, I went out there to get a job falling off horses in cowboy and Indian movies, but when I got there"—he winked at Forbes—"Italians already had all the jobs."

Forbes took a long pull on the beer that he had intended for Red Horse.

"Well, that's Hollywood for you." Forbes took a sip from the other beer can, seemingly quite unaware that he was drinking from both cans of beer. "It has the courage of its own lack of convictions. But remember, my old friend, I gave you a job. I gave you your chance. It didn't matter to me if you were a . . ."

Red Horse interrupted. "I lied to get the job."

Forbes choked, mid-gulp, and beer dribbled down his chin.

"What?"

"I told you I was Italian."

"Uh, really?" Forbes tried to remember, looking somewhat confused. "Uh, I thought that . . . uh . . ."

"You didn't find out I was really an Indian until our third film, *Son of the Apache Devil.* I was the only one who didn't get a sunburn. That's how you found out."

Forbes shook his head, suddenly remembering. "Now I remember. I always said you rode a horse too good to be an Italian."

He tilted his head back, drained the beer intended for Red Horse. He shook the can to make sure it was empty, then tossed it over his shoulder. It banged against the back wall of the cabin.

Red Horse had almost risen out of his chair, as if his body had been trying to follow the path of the beer can. There was a look of abject longing on his face. He eyed the paper bag at Forbes's feet with hope and expectation.

One-handed, Forbes stuck a cigarette in his mouth and lit it, unaware of Red Horse's distress.

Forbes coughed rackingly, with the first inhalation of the cigarette. He looked over at Red Horse.

"So you faked it a little at a time when everybody faked it a lot. So what? It doesn't matter now. The point is, I kept you on. I made you the first Indian star of the shoot-'em-ups. And I hired more real Indians in my films than any other director." He had another coughing fit, which he soothed with a swig of beer from the other can. "You can't take that away from me."

"What's to take? I always figured the Great Spirit gave you your chance to direct motion pictures. It was the Great Spirit who chose you to make so many Westerns about Indians."

Forbes almost choked on his beer.

"For a second there, I thought you might actually be complimenting me on something."

Red Horse nodded slyly as if in agreement. "I think you were the Great Spirit's choice."

Forbes finished the second beer, and shook the empty can. "Thanks, Red Horse. I'm truly flattered."

"The Great Spirit would have wanted somebody who wasn't going to mess it up by knowing anything."

Forbe's hand tightened around his cigarette, snapping it off behind the filter. He realized he had been had.

"You talk more than any Indian I ever met."

He paused for emphasis.

"Talk is silver."

He took a long dramatic pause, broken only by the sound of the empty beer can rattling off the wall as he flipped it over his shoulder. Then he spoke.

"BUT SILENCE IS GOLDEN!"

Red Horse's body again unconsciously tracked the flight of the beer can.

He answered. "And a fart is nobody's friend. Let's have ANOTHER goddamn beer!"

Forbes nodded in agreement with the sentiment. He started to bend over and had another coughing spasm which left him gasping for breath, pale and shaken. He looked over at Red Horse. "You don't really like me, do you?"

He averted his eyes then and reached down and got two more beers out of the bag. He held the cans in his lap, keeping his eyes on them.

Red Horse took the corncob pipe out of his mouth slowly and cradled it in the palm of his hand as if it suddenly were very heavy. He looked suddenly very weary.

Forbes went on, "When I think of all the years, all the things we went through. Out on location in the middle of a thousand nowheres, not quite in hell and no ways near heaven. Seems like I spent two whole lifetimes with you . . . and with your people." He opened both cans slowly as if the act helped him shape his thoughts. "I made it possible for you to live in a better way. I gave you money. I gave you fame even. And even though it was Hollywood all the way where everything is bent, I think I pretty damn near always was straight with you."

Red Horse nodded. "In that I agree. In Hollywood, honest meant undetected. But you were straight with me in your heart."

Forbes settled back deeper into the rocking chair, extended a can of beer to Red Horse and said, "So how come, that being true . . . all those years . . . you never took my hand in friendship?"

Red Horse, his hand about to close on the beer, said, "Maybe because there was always the rustle of paper money when your hand came out."

Angry, Forbes withdrew his hand, letting the beer can come back to rest in his lap.

Red Horse lunged futilely at the can of beer.

Forbes bolted a gulp of beer angrily, from the can he had been offering to Red Horse.

Red Horse balled his hand into a fist, as if he wished to take a poke at Forbes, but thinking better of it, unclenched his hand.

"You don't need to take it so personal. There was always one more take, one more horse to fall off of. I never did anything for you that I wasn't paid for. That is a difficult way to live."

Forbes drank again from Red Horse's beer and then said, "I never cheated you. I was generous. I paid you what you were worth and then some. A man can look back on that with pride, can't he?"

Red Horse watched him drink, licking his lips.

"What I did you always asked me to do for money, you never asked me to do it for you because I was your friend."

Forbes waved both cans of beer for emphasis. "Christ! I didn't want to take advantage of our friendship!"

"Until you do something to test it, friendship has no strength. It has no heart until you risk it."

Forbes started to hand the can of beer to Red Horse as if suddenly remembering that it was his beer.

"I held back," and Forbes, unaware of the action, drew back the can just as Red Horse lunged for it, "because I respected you."

"You can't expect that of friends in this life. Respect is only good after you are dead. Then you hope your friends don't let their horses stand too long over your grave."

Forbes grimaced and downed the rest of Red Horse's beer. "Well, you give me a pain in the . . ."

Red Horse, half angry about the past and half angry about the beer, cut in. "Don't tell me pain stories. I fell off three hundred and fifty horses of a different Technicolor. I rode across your screen. I danced for you. I fell off horses for you. I got shot for you. I was living in two worlds and the Great Spirit was working the night shift. When you said do a rain dance, I did a rain dance." He banged his corncob pipe angrily against the wooden arm of the rocking chair. "When the script called for a woman, you changed me into one. Don't tell me about pain!"

"I feel pain too. Like the one in my heart right now. I always liked you. . . . Always. . . . You treat me badly. Would it break your red rear end to admit to liking me, even a little? Just once, maybe, for old times' sakes?"

Red Horse smiled cagily. "Supposing I did like you, always did like you, I wouldn't tell you."

"It isn't fair. I'm always getting the shaft. I guess I shot too many movies and not enough actors."

"Being liked is something that is known and doesn't have to be told," said Red Horse.

The white man looked unhappy. "We all like to be liked. What's the harm in saying it?"

The Indian shook his head. "Plenty harm. All these years, you are the same man who drank the water. You never changed. If it wasn't a cattle stampede or dynamiting the dam, you couldn't feel it. If I saw a hundred people on horseback, I looked for someone I knew. You worried if they had taken their wristwatches off or whether or not the horses would do something unfortunate on camera when they rode by. I looked for a home in every face I saw. But what did you look for?"

"I was always looking for the big picture," said Forbes defensively.

"There was never a big picture. Only big people with hearts as big as the sky, for the man who had time to see it."

"I must be crazy, talking about movies to you. You never sat in the director's chair. I had to move mountains. I had to play God!"

Forbes had a dreamy sort of look on his face. "In the beginning, was montage. Then it was an endless parade of forty-nine-year-old starlets in soft focus who had never been kissed. I was a good director! Hell, I was a great director because I was lonely. Because in that silence that surrounded me, I chased the greatest loneliness of all, that a man can aspire to. I moved and shaked. My power was in my ability to motivate, to show the donkey the carrot."

He drank from the other can of beer.

Red Horse eyed the beer can and said, "You never had it so good."

"Or parted with it so fast. Yes sir, Red Horse, you're a genius in Hollywood, until you lose your job."

Red Horse looked at the bowl of his pipe. "Well, life is a choice of choices. You could have ridden some other horse, chased some other sunset."

Forbes shook his head. "I don't think so. I didn't know anything else. Didn't want to know anything else. A director is a guy who aims at something he can't see and hits it if he's lucky with bullets from empty guns." He finished his beer and tossed the can away. "A director has certain responsibilities."

"A human being only has one. Being human."

"I could never explain my life to you, Red Horse."

"It's not my job to understand your life. That's the white woman's burden," said Red Horse solemnly.

"Leave my ex-wife out of this," said Forbes wearily.

"Even so, I always understood you. You wanted to hit the big jackpot which meant you had to become a slug in the machine. You wanted to get into the big poker game of the ages but you bluffed with the same hand for too long. They brought in a new dealer and your Westerns fell off the same horse I once rode. A six-gun stopped beating four of a kind."

Forbes stared at the old Indian with simulated disgust. "You are a philosopher. That is not good. They'll say you use drugs."

Forbes threw the last beer can over his shoulder. Red Horse winced as it bounced noisily off the wall.

"I WOULD if I could get any." He stared down at the bag in front of Forbes's chair with longing. "But beer is up another dollar a six-pack. I say the world is coming to an end."

Forbes nodded in half-drunken agreement. "Have another beer, Red Horse."

Red Horse sighed. "Maybe you should stop being so generous with my beer."

Forbes took out two more cans of beer, set them in his lap and began to open them. His fingers were now very unsteady. He paused from this task to put another cigarette in his mouth. Red Horse leaned over and lit the cigarette for him.

Forbes thanked him with a nod, took a few puffs and then had such a violent coughing fit, the cigarette flew out of his mouth.

Forbes bent over, tears in his eyes, barely able to breathe. "I didn't have to be a film director. I could have been a gynecologist."

Red Horse agreed. "Cowboys and Indians can't last forever but women are something the world can't live without."

Forbes shook his head with regret. "I used to have a real personality but a producer got rid of it for me. I spent a lot of time working for people who tried to put my head in a wine bottle."

"You should have quit when it started to fit," said Red Horse.

Forbes announced decisively, "Another beer. Just the thing to wash the rotten taste of Hollywood out of our mouths."

"At least I wasn't a Hollywood phony. People hated me for myself."

Forbes drank from the can in his left hand, nodded in satisfaction and then treated himself to another gulp, this time from the can in the other hand that he had just opened for Red Horse.

Red Horse sighed. "My generosity knows no bounds."

"Forty years a director. I spent most of my life in half-lit rooms with half-lit people. I was drunk on success, drunk on money, drunk on power . . . and I was drunk, too. And then, right into the toilet. I went from the house on the hill to the phone booth on the corner of walk and don't walk. It should have meant more than that."

"I always said the same thing about your films."

"What's wrong with my films, you drunken old totem pole!"

"Aside from me being in them, everything else is what is wrong with them."

Forbes gestured with the beer cans, angrily spilling some of the beer.

"You take that back! My films were true to life. They meant something! They were steeped in authenticity!"

"They were steeped in something," admitted Red Horse.

Forbes acknowledged, "Oh, I may have cut a few corners here and there but I attempted to depict what I could see."

"A crazy man and a not crazy man think the same way. The difference is where you start."

Forbes gestured even more wildly, spilling more beer. "If you didn't like my films, if you didn't believe in the . . . in the moral integrity of my films, why did you stay all these years?"

"I didn't have to believe in your films, only your money. You had the most believable money I ever saw."

Forbes smashed the beer cans against his chest, spraying himself with beer. "Let me tell you something, you miserable model for a buffalo nickel, I had to believe in them. Every producer insisted, so he wouldn't have to. I sweated out every word uttered in every one of my films." Contemptuously, Forbes flung the half-filled beer cans over his shoulder, spraying both of them in a fine shower of beer. "What other director can say that?"

Red Horse wiped beer off his face, and looked disgusted. "Kissing yourself above the knees is hard work."

"Remember that death scene in *They Rode Bold for Gold*? You helped me write it yourself! You can't tell me that scene didn't have something!"

Forbes was very much caught up in the memory, making elaborately drunken gestures with his hands. "The faithful Indian returning to warn his white master of the ambush, only to drop dead at his feet. I said to you, 'Red Horse, you gasp out your words of warning in English, then look far away into the distance and say your dying words in your own tongue. Thinking of your wife and child back at the wigwam, never to see them again. You gave your all for the white man but your heart returned to your people at the last moment.' It was your greatest moment on screen and it wasn't even in English. I did that. I insisted that the last words you spoke should be Indian. I made it authentic. It was just the right touch. I had the audiences crying in their socks! Remember! It was so successful I had you do it in all the other movies."

"You also said not to say it in real Indian. You just wanted to make it sound Indian."

"I said that?"

"I wouldn't forget something like that."

Forbes frowned. "Well, so what? It's the thought that counted. It sounded Indian. Nobody could tell it wasn't Indian. I didn't want to offend any particular Indian tribe. I had producers to answer to."

"I could tell. My people could tell. Which is why I went ahead and said it in my own language anyway."

"You what? You did what?"

"In my death scene, I spoke my own language."

Forbes stared darkly at him, rebuke on his face. "If I had

known, I'd have skinned you alive. No director has to take that kind of insubordination."

"Aren't you curious to know what I really said?"

Forbes shrugged. "It was a death scene, the highest point in the film. I'm sure you said something appropriate."

Red Horse deliberately spoke in the stiff, unnatural Indianese of the old bad Westerns. "Translated, it went like this. 'No. This . . . not . . . arrow in my stomach. I just excited.' "

Forbes spread his hands to the heavens above as if inviting a lightning bolt to put him out of his misery. "And to think, I wasted a whole lifetime liking you. I should have stuck with the Italians. They ride horses like old people make love but they don't shaft you when you're NOT looking."

Red Horse snorted derisively. "They only shaft you when you ARE looking."

"Red Horse, you're the kind of guy who takes a sack full of kittens down to the river to drown them and then starts to cry," he said wickedly, "because you can't get them to skip."

He pointed an accusing finger at Red Horse's chest.

"What did I ever do to you, anyway? Is it because a lot of Indians think you're an Uncle Tomahawk because of the films you made with me? Is that what you're holding against me? Are you blaming me because some people think you're some kind of stupid wooden Indian Hollywood clown?"

"I enjoy being a clown. That is my sanity. If you laugh you survive death, if you don't you die out. To be an Indian and to be too serious is to be blind and trapped in the white man's frantic world where death is not an old friend, just a terrifying interruption."

"I take what I do seriously, what I have done. In Europe, they still watch my old films. They call me a great artist. They appreciate my vision, my sensitivity."

"To be appreciated. That is a very serious hell. It is a power too strong to be overcome by anything except flight."

Forbes said defensively, "I put things on film that had never been seen before. I spent my whole life at it. It had to mean something to you, to your people."

"Your films landed where the hands of man never set foot."

"I sought truth."

"You could have had the dreams locked in men's hearts. The dreams of my people. You could have had my hand in friendship. That is all the truth a man need know."

"I helped keep your people alive. I created visions of your life, maybe not accurate in every detail, but the meaning was there. I gave the world moments of your people's lives for all to see."

"You may have shown the world how we might have lived and behaved but never how we thought or felt. The fire you lit for us, flashed and flared and danced on the silver screen but showed us only the dark in which we lived."

Forbes was overcome with a sudden, convulsive fit of coughing. It left him looking very ill and old and worn out. He looked at the old Indian next to him and there was pain in his eyes that was not from the illness inside him.

"All these years, have you hated me?"

"Could I hate you when the whole world was watching? You always had the courage to make a fool of yourself and then you were willing to take the rest of the world with you. I never felt exploited or used. Mostly I was amazed at your earnest stupidity."

Red Horse looked into Forbes's eyes, understanding the pain there.

"I was born a savage. You called me forth from my reservation prison, dressed me up as a Noble Savage or a vicious one, taught me to ride horses I couldn't afford to own and to pretend to kill men I had no reason to hate.

"I put away the cowboy boots that really fit and wore the costumer's moccasins that didn't fit and never would.

"I danced dances for the camera that meant nothing, chanted chants even I didn't understand, scalped bald men and endlessly rode in a circle around Western Civilization.

"You always said you were looking for truth but instead I always thought you were looking for some purity in my primitiveness.

"You called me forth in a hundred different costumes no man of my tribe would have been caught dead in, painted like devils too evil for us to even dream of.

"You brought me and my people exotic and disguised onto

the silver screen in every shape and color and flavor of reality but our own. And why?

"Every time I fell off a horse when a white man shot his six-shooter for the seventh time, I always asked myself what was in it for you.

"Then one day I figured it out.

"I was a guilty pleasure. I was something suppressed in your own life. I and my people were an experience, civilized white people are denied the luxury of indulging in.

"So we were summoned forth but our reality didn't match your forbidden fantasy . . . so you recast, rewrote, recut and reclothed the missing part of your heart's forbidden desires, thereby giving the rest of the world a chance to satisfy its own deepest secret fears.

"Some of my people called me Uncle Tomahawk because I danced for you. Because I got shot for you, because I always fell off horses so beautifully for you.

"But I seduced the world with your foolish help. I gave the world an interesting lie. I kept truth for myself."

"How could you live a lie?" said Forbes, shocked.

"How could you film one?" said Red Horse with a smile.

"I was approximating a truth. I felt it to be true. I had my beliefs in some of it. I was cynical, God knows. I gave the hicks what they wanted to see. I never disappointed my audience. Well, not for a long time anyway. Later I lost control of myself and lost my grip on the audience too."

Red Horse turned and looked at the empty beer cans on the floor. "Drinking wore away the first half of your strength."

Forbes agreed. "My ex-wife, who fancied herself, considered herself entitled to the second half. I did my last films with what was left."

"I still don't know how you spent your whole life chasing a truth that would not fit in your hand or heart."

Forbes was looking at something outside the room, as if he were staring at his own past. "Maybe because I was in love, in love with all the faces in the dark I never knew. Maybe because I thought when I found my audience, I would somehow find myself. When I touched them, I would touch me.

"Maybe because people were too full of feelings I couldn't express in me, because I could be content with an image.

"I was looking for a place to die on the photograph of my soul. I lived like some kind of deranged ghoul who put cameras in Geronimo's coffin in order to interview Indian worms.

"Sometimes I think I am an evil old man because I chased a truth about a people who wouldn't tell it to me, because I wanted selfishly to put it all in one stunning montage, in one brilliant symbolic lap dissolve, seeing you and your people chained to my wishes, turning from untamed bodies dancing on trees to a pair of eyes staring beautifully in the dark."

"You are a dying man. It is in your voice. It is in your eyes." Red Horse reached out and put his arm around Forbes's shoulder. "This is a good joke. It is all behind you. It is up to other people to stumble upon new lies. You will make no more films, my old friend, and that is well and just, for I do not wish to fall off any more horses."

Forbes's voice trembled with emotion. "I've got cancer. I just came to say good-bye. I don't have much time."

Red Horse smiled. He seemed strangely cheerful at the news. "I too am nearing my time. Big parts of my body are ready to fall off. It is a hell of a good joke. We can race and see which one falls apart first.

"I was beginning to get angry at you. I have been waiting up for you. I have been saving up some of the most interesting lies, also lots of dirty stories.

"I have been holding off on the dying business, waiting for you to catch up. If you think I am going to fall off three hundred and fifty goddamn horses of a different Technicolor for you and get bumps and bruises and damaged parts for every damn inch of me, having gone through all that, then die all alone, you're crazy!

"We are old and out of horses. We are past sex and the arrogance of it. We have lived a lifetime together and the hurts and lies of the past are not only over, they are forgiven.

"All our lives, we have loved each other, as friends, as human beings.

"I have always known this because I am Indian but you have

only suspected it because you are white and stupid and as crazy as three ducks with wooden legs trying to be quiet.

"Now it is right that we will be together at the end. I am glad you did not stay in Hollywood, to die among strangers. What I cannot understand, is what took you so long to get here. I almost had to sit on matches all day long just to keep the heart fire lit."

Forbes smiled. "I had to help my ex-wife get her cat down out of a tree. The reason I'm late is because I'm such a poor shot."

"You always were a gentleman. You never hit a woman with your hat on."

Forbes tried to hide the tears leaking from the corners of his eyes. He tried to straighten his back, get a grip on himself. "What gets me . . . I . . . all these years . . . what I tried to do . . . tried to say . . . how I carried myself . . . I was so . . . so damn afraid you wouldn't like me. Goddamn, I tried so damn hard to be your friend. . . . I hoped . . . why am I so goddamned dim that I have to wait till the last reel to find out the truth?"

"The truth only waits for eyes not filled with longing."

There was a silence between the two of them. The thought hung in the air between them, like a bridge that spanned an old, deep river they had always longed to cross.

Forbes bent over and got out two cans of beer. They were the last two cans in the sack. He opened them, held them in his lap, a can in each hand. Red Horse was staring at him, his hands balled into fists.

Forbes peered into the growing darkness of the day and said, "I think the matinee is almost over. We didn't ride off into the sunset and we didn't get the girl."

The old Indian put his pipe in his shirt pocket with an air of putting it away forever. "I died in a hundred movies and I never felt like I feel now that I'm actually doing it."

"If it feels like you've had to go to the bathroom for five years, and can't, you and me are in the same movie," said Forbes.

"Death may turn out to be funny. I hope not too damn funny. If there is a happy hunting ground and we go there, John Forbes, it better by Christ not be a movie set."

Forbes started to take a drink from Red Horse's beer.

"Hell, don't worry about it. If it is, you're a personal friend of the director, and we'll get ourselves a rewrite." He lifted Red Horse's can of beer to his lips. "I already got a good idea how to redo our death scene."

Red Horse lunged forward and grabbed his arm at the wrist.

He said, "There is no death, only a change of worlds." He snatched the beer can out of Forbes's hands. "AND IN THE NEXT WORLD, BRING SOME OF YOUR OWN DAMN BEER."

The Game of Cat and Eagle

The Marine band played the Air Force hymn loud enough to scare the eagle.

He wasn't happy in the cage anyway—no eagle ever is.

When I stepped off the chopper at Camranh Bay, the caged eagle under my arm made me conspicuous.

Colonel Ranklin, a very correct soldier, impeccably starched, met me with a jeep at the end of the pier. The smell of the harbor, a heavy tang of oil and salt water mingled with sewage, struck my nostrils.

"I have orders to take you to your next transport," said Colonel Ranklin, saluting smartly.

There was a look of displeasure on his face. He expected possibly high brass, or somebody with a high covert status, anything but a long-haired Indian with a caged eagle.

I got into the jeep, glad to drop the cage. I had a couple of wounds where the eagle had got at me through the bars.

"You are the Mystery Guest?"

"I guess so. I've got a name, too—call me Lookseeker. You can't blame the code name on me. They always make a game out of everything."

"Right," said Colonel Ranklin, climbing into the jeep. He threw the jeep into gear and we were off. He never looked back, driving at a half-slow and very cautious pace through the dock area. We threaded our way through what seemed like millions of tons of military cargo, awaiting transshipment.

He kept his back straight; perhaps he had been born with a back like that, formed to fit against the wall.

There was a coldness about him I didn't like, and he hadn't asked for proper identification or shown his own, either.

They had issued me a standard sidearm, but I had turned it in. Where the eagle and I were going, guns wouldn't help. But now, pondering the silent figure driving the jeep, I felt threatened and wished I had a weapon.

We went past a large storage shed and he turned the wheel abruptly to the right.

Two men lounging beside the shed sprang into action. They jerked on ropes and a steel shuttered door slid up. The jeep slowed, righted itself, and we shot into the open doorway.

As soon as we had made it inside, the heavy doors clanged shut behind us with a bang.

The lights went on, flooding the dimly lit interior with blazing light.

A tall man in a business suit sat on a chair, flanked by heavily armed men of the 315th Air Commando Group.

My driver got out of the jeep and walked away, not looking back. He lit a cigarette and strolled behind a stack of ammo cases.

"Don't bother getting out of the jeep, Lookseeker," said the man in civilian clothes. "I won't keep you very long."

"Who are you? Why am I being detained?"

The man winced. "Hardly detained. Let us say, momentarily delayed. I'm Hightower. I'm with the CIA."

"Somehow, I'm not surprised," I said.

"You know, this is a war we could win. I want you to know that I honestly believe that. I don't think I would like to see it end prematurely. We still need more time."

I studied him. He had a lean face, a killer's face, but a kind of sadness suffused his features. He projected a fatherly aura, radiating charm and warmth that probably did not exist.

"What does this have to do with me?" I asked. The eagle shrieked and flung itself at the bars of its cage as it had done many times before.

He smiled and I felt a cold wind, as if something had stirred the air above a grave. "Let us say that civilized as we may seem, America is no more civilized than we choose to be. Do we make war with logic and precision and science? The Pentagon would have us believe so. But you and I, Lookseeker, we know differently. Hitler had his astrologers. Eisenhower had a rabbit foot in his pocket throughout the war. War brings out the mystic need for answers in the most civilized men."

"I am surprised. You seem to know what my mission is. I was told that no one would know," I said and I knew this was truly a dangerous man. And a dying man as well. I could feel it, almost see it glowing beneath his skin, an unstoppable cancer, a shadow riotously burgeoning with dark unlife.

"How I know is unimportant. But make no mistake about it, my friend, I am deeply concerned by what you are about to do. I don't like it. I detest it just as I detest all of the tired old mystical, religious mumbo jumbo of the past. I am an irreligious man. Winning is my religion."

"If you were to ask me, I would say you are a very religious man," I said, borrowing some of the eagle's wisdom. "If you were not, you would not so deeply fear what I am about to do."

The man jerked as if struck. His face grayed and he looked down at his hands. They were white, long and pale, like blind worms from a subterranean cave. There was a pallor about the man that suggested that he seldom saw the sun, sitting like a spider in his dark web, spinning dark nets to entrap his prey.

"Perhaps you are right," he said and he looked at me strangely. "You are not what I expected."

He looked at me carefully, as if trying to figure out just how dangerous I was by the way I looked.

I did not make an intimidating figure. I have long, black, very unmilitary hair. I am not tall, neither am I particularly handsome. My face is too thin, my eyes are too large with things that walk through the thousand thousand dark nights of man. The military uniform I wore was much too big for me. Hollywood would never have cast me as a warrior or a medicine man. In my own way, though, I was both.

"I think you expected to see an old man, rattling skulls and waving feathers and chanting mysterious chants. Something like that."

"Yes." His smile was almost real now. "Perhaps, if you looked like a fake, I might be more inclined to dismiss you as a childish whim on his part."

"What do you want with me? I don't think you have the authority to stop me, if that's what you've got in mind."

"I could kill you," he said smoothly, his tone devoid of menace. "A sniper. This area is hit so often with snipers, we call them duty snipers. I could arrange it."

Colonel Ranklin had returned. He seemed nervous, a cigarette burning in the corner of his mouth. I noticed he had one hand on the butt of his sidearm.

"I'm sure you could," I said and then I lost all fear of Hightower, suddenly knowing he was just scared. Terrified. Of me, of what I stood for.

I motioned to Colonel Ranklin. "Let's go, driver. We've wasted enough time here."

Hightower stood up, moving angrily toward the jeep. He put his hand on the door of the jeep, his mouth set in a grim line.

"I haven't said you could go yet. I haven't decided if you'll ever go."

"Yes, you have." I felt sorry for him. "Because you want to know the answer as badly as the man who sent me. You'd kill me because you wanted to change the answer, that I believe, but you'd never kill me knowing that I may be the only one who can reveal the answer. You are more afraid of not knowing than knowing."

Colonel Ranklin now had his weapon out.

Hightower turned and looked back at him. Ranklin waited for an order.

"Drive him," said Hightower.

Ranklin looked disappointed as he reholstered his gun. The heavy doors went up and Ranklin got back into the jeep.

Hightower put his hand on my arm, like a supplicant seeking favor from the gods. "Don't tell anyone I talked to you. I'd appreciate it." The sadness was on his face again.

"Who would I tell," I said as the jeep began backing out of the shed. "I never met you, and if anyone asks why we're late, I'll tell them Colonel Ranklin stopped to pay a visit to a whorehouse to pick up his laundry and have his back ironed straight in the usual military fashion."

I heard Hightower laughing as we drove away. Even laughing, the man sounded scared.

Ranklin never spoke again. I knew he was a skilled assassin, and looking at him, I looked to see how he would die. The great lizard spoke to me and I saw Ranklin in a bar, drinking with a Vietnamese whore. He thought she loved him.

I looked up and saw a Vietnamese woman pull the pin from a grenade and toss it into the club. To save the girl, Ranklin fell on the grenade. It was a good death for an assassin. A little honor for a man who had none.

I made my next transport in time. Another chopper. On board, I fed the eagle another chunk of raw meat. Ungrateful, the eagle expressed a preference for my fingers as I tried to thrust the meat through the bars of the cage.

The eagle and I are not friends. My totem and my vision ally is a lizard, the Ancient of Reptiles, the eagle's enemy. Perhaps the eagle senses this and regards me as its enemy, perhaps I am simply contaminated with too much contact with men.

The unrelenting heat seemed to strike against us as the chopper sped toward my next jumping-off place.

The chopper pilot noticed my discomfort. "Welcome to Sauna City," he said, waving his thumb to the left toward Da Nang as we passed near it. "At noon, you can fry rice in your helmet while you're wearing it."

"Any advice for a new recruit?" I asked. The chopper pilot looked at my dark skin, dark eyes, and slightly built body in the uniform at least a size too big for me.

"You'll pardon me saying so," he said in a lazy Texas drawl, "but you ain't exactly sporting a military look with the hair there, sport. Now I see lots of long hair, after you've parked here for a while, but you're the first greenie to arrive with it. You must be an Indian or a Mexican."

"I could plead guilty to one of those," I said, looking back to see how the eagle was taking to the chopper ride. He seemed fairly quiet. I found that strapping his cage near an open door seemed to make him content. The air rushing in must have made him think he was flying. "So what?"

"If I were you, Tonto or Pronto or whichever you are, I'd practice looking as white as possible. Over here the weirdness swallows you. It's best to look like just one side, not two."

We had arrived at our destination. I meant to ask him what he meant by that statement but he got busy landing us, so I let it ride. He hunched forward over the controls as he brought the chopper in. I saw the spot on his back where the flak would catch him and tear his insides out.

I jumped out the door of the chopper as soon as we touched down.

"Eagle for eating or do you ride it around?" said the pilot as he began handing down the cage to me.

"This not eagle, white boy, this is Texas chicken," I said with a grin.

The pilot touched the door frame of the chopper. "Hell, boy, you just rode in a Texas chicken! That scrawny thing . . ." The eagle got him by the hand and bit down hard. "Christ! He cut me to the bone!" moaned the pilot, holding his bloody hand. "Good luck, Chief, and thanks for the Purple Heart!"

"First blood," I said under my breath to the eagle with a smile on my face and turned to look around at my surroundings. Behind me, the chopper lifted off, driving the eagle in the cage wild again.

I was on the helipad at Tan Son Nhut Air Base, temporarily assigned as a door gunner to the 145th. At least, that was the paperwork designation that hid my real mission there.

I heard a high-pitched whine and turned to see an F-100 taxi by on an adjacent runway. I wondered what the hell the chopper pilot had meant by what he had said. The weirdness swallows you? How does one look like one side and not two? I hadn't spoken it aloud, just thought it, but a voice answered, "He meant you look too Vietnamese." This came from a pilot sitting in the cockpit of a blunt-nosed Super Sabre. "And you can bet your brown rear end, that's no real asset here. Sure as hell, some trigger-happy cowboy is going to nail your ass thinking you're a VC infiltrator in a good-guy suit. Maybe you ought to curl your hair. Maybe they'll think you're a Jew with a severe tan." The pilot laughed. "Christ, I'm getting almost too funny to live!"

"How could you have heard what the chopper pilot said to me over the whine of the rotors? And how did you know I didn't understand what he meant?"

"Welcome to Vietnam. It ain't what people say that you got to hear, it's what they don't say that counts," said the pilot, giving me a double thumbs up and a wink.

I spotted the chopper that was to take me to Bien Hoa.

I turned to say thanks for the advice, lame as it was, to the pilot in the Super Sabre, but the plane was gone. Where it had stood was a burned hulk of a jet in a mortar crater. The wreckage was at least six months old.

In spirit quests, by the Sacred Lake of my people, after long fasts and much suffering, I have seen animal spirits that were not there, and sometimes the dead spoke to me. But never in the real world have the dead spoken to me.

I looked all around me then and I saw that I was in a place that was unlike itself. I looked in the old ways of my people, where a tree stood I saw not the tree but its shadow. This was a shadow world, half robed in the strange clothes of the dead, and alive only with things of another world.

I approached the chopper I had been ordered to report to, staggering under the weight of cage and eagle. A line of bullet holes ran across the middle of the craft. Somebody had stuck plastic roses in the holes.

I knew the pilot, by name at least.

I saluted stiffly.

Lieutenant Colonel J. N. Howton regarded me with a strange look on his face. "Can the salute, pinhead! You must be Lieutenant Lookseeker. What the hell is it you do, boy? The brass said you were a very hush-hush secret weapon."

"I'm sorry. I have been instructed to say that the information you have requested is classified."

Howton jumped out of his craft, circling it. "OK, high-hat me, I don't give a shit. Just get your classified ass in the chopper. I'm preflighting it. It won't take long—just a few extra minutes of insurance. You a weapons specialist?"

"I have been instructed to say . . ." I began.

"Aw, shut the hell up with that crap, will ya," he growled. "Stow your equipment on board. If you don't know much about choppers, climb topside with me and I'll fill you in. Also, you can count the bullet holes on your side. If we come up with the magic number, we win a magic elephant, personally autographed by General Westmoreland himself."

I stowed the cage in the back and then I climbed up after him. He pointed out the rotor head, and then indicated a large retaining nut which holds the rotors to the mast.

"Just thought I'd tell you, this dingus keeps it flying. If this whatsis comes off, we lose the blades and we take on the aerodynamic capabilities of a pregnant rock. We call the dingus the Jesus nut."

"It won't come off," I said. "A Russian surface-to-air missile will down this chopper and fuse it in place."

"What did you say?" Howton had a strange look on his face.

I turned away. I had spoken before I thought. So often with me, I say things that I wish I could keep inside. But as these things so easily spring to my mind, also so easily do they spring to my lips.

"You're a strange one, Lookseeker," said Howton. "How many bullet holes on your side?"

"I count ten, eleven, uh, fourteen," I said.

"Damn, there's only twenty-two on my side. Never going to break no damn records this way," said Howton with a good-natured curse.

We climbed down and entered into the chopper.

I was already wearing a flak vest, but once inside the chopper, Howton insisted that I put on a fifteen-pound chest protector of laminated steel and plastic.

"Bet you never thought you'd ever be wearing an iron brassiere," said Howton as he buckled himself in at the controls. The crew chief and door gunner fitted ammo belts into their M-60 machine guns. I was given a flight helmet and settled it on my head. I adjusted my headset so I could hear the radio transmission between our craft and Saigon ground control.

"Helicopter Nine Nine Four. Departure from Hotel Three. East departure mid-field crossing." That was what Howton said into the radio. What I heard was Howton's life twisting in the dark like a lost white bird. I heard his heart stop in the crash that was yet to be and almost cried out because though Howton's heart died with no pain, it caused a hole between the two worlds of home and here, and the hole let the dark wind in.

All my life, I have feared the dark winds.

In a strongly Vietnamese-accented voice, Saigon control replied, "Roger, Nine Nine Four. Takeoff approved. We have you for a cross at five hundred feet."

We lifted with a thump, hovered over the adjoining runway,

our nose tilted down, and then there was a larger thump as we went through transitional lift and soared up and away.

"Your first eyeball of the terrain?" asked Howton over the roar of the blades. "Or did you scope it on the flight in?"

I looked down at the land which I knew I would leave my bones in. I did not see what Howton saw. I saw the flat tabletop lands of my people, the great stone mesas, the pueblos gleaming in the shimmering heat.

I didn't speak. Howton dropped the chopper until we were flying just above the treetops. "Why are we flying so low?"

"Heavy VC batteries in this section. I'm not cleared for the upper lane, so if I can't go high, I go as low as I can get it. Harder to hit us. Our exposure time is shorter this way."

The UH-1D chopper vibrated a lot as we skirted the treetops. Two gunships joined up with us, taking up position on each side of us.

The radio crackled, giving off a brief series of orders in code which I did not recognize. It was half in code, half in slang.

Howton spoke into his headset. "This is Hownow Howton. Nine Nine Four. I'd like permission to divert to extradite ARVNs at Phu Loi."

"Negative. Continue with mission," was the immediate reply.

Howton regarded me sourly. He glanced upward—the sky was filling with jets, F-100s.

He began a rapid upward climb.

"Your nursemaids are here. Time to take the high road."

"Wish I knew what the hell it is you do," said Howton. "You're becoming an itch I can't scratch."

We gained a fairly high altitude, paced by the gunships on each side and the ever-present jets.

"You're a short-timer," I said to Howton. "Your wife, Annie, loves you very much."

"Don't recall mentioning her name, Chief. Somebody brief you on me or what? Maybe you're one of those psychic types?" Howton regarded me with cynical distrust.

"I just know things," I said.

"Not in this case, partner," said Howton, hunched over the controls. "I've got a big four hundred and thirty-eight days to go. A long hard winter and a long hard summer and another goddamn winter to boot. Sort of like a two-for-one sale."

At times like this, when I know too much, I find myself growing quiet and cold and remote from life. Remote and cold because there is nothing I can do for those around me. Knowledge of what is yet to be is not always a way to change what is about to become.

I knew in less than ten days Lieutenant Colonel J. N. Howton would die in a fiery helicopter crash. I knew his wife, Annie, who hated war, would slowly drink herself to death and would know no other men in her life. And so, two lives would burn in the crash of a helicopter in this place of shadows.

Howton spoke into his headset, talking to the bay-door gunner. "What's the good word from the back of the bus?"

"This is Doctor Death, in basic black, here, talking the stuff at you, big pilot. I got zero unfriendlies. I got Rattlers on my sleeves and we is A-fine and Butt Ugly." Doctor Death was a huge black with gold teeth. Huge muscles threatened to burst the shoulders out of his olive-drab T-shirt. He wore a baseball cap decorated with chicken feathers and a huge button that said, I LIKE IKE. HE'S DEAD.

"That's the meanest son of a bitch who ever squatted over a quad 7.62 machine gun. They tell me he shot his mother. Claimed she was a VC infiltrator."

"He'll survive the war but not the heroin," I said and then wished I hadn't said it. I hadn't meant to.

Howton shook his head. "You are a little too weird to live, if you ask me, Big Chief. How about you do me and mine a favor and lay off the heavy gloom and doom."

"Sure." I grinned at him. "Maybe it's just Indians are naturally pessimistic. Probably has something to do with losing a whole continent."

"Hey! How come I gots to ride shotgun on this here wild-ass chicken? The damn thing just bit the hell out of me!" said Doctor Death.

"That's an eagle, numb butt! It's on the cargo manifest and it's classified top secret, so keep your paws off it! It's worth more than you are on this mission," snapped Howton.

I could tell Howton wanted to ask me about the eagle but perhaps he knew I couldn't tell him anything.

"Listen, since I am going to be the last to know, maybe you can tell me what kind of traffic we're heading for?" asked Howton.

"I know even less than you do. All I know is, I'm to join up with a unit called the 145th, at a place called Phu Loi."

"You ain't been out to fight no war yet, Big Chief. You smell green to me. So where do they get off calling you a secret weapon? You some kind of superskunk? Is that it, Big Chief—you lift your legs and squirt smell juice on old Uncle Ho Chi Minh?"

"I've donated blood on a battlefield on another world," I said, but I knew it was not something I could explain.

"Yeah, well you're a freaking Martian and I'm Doctor Death's toothless old mother," said Howton, scanning the horizon. "This is it. Our landing zone."

"Where are we exactly?"

"As the cootie flies, we're northwest of Saigon, near the Michelin Rubber Plantation, if that tells you anything."

We landed on the helipad. Howton turned in his seat, looked at me expectantly. "Now what?"

The radio kicked in. "Nine Nine Four. This is Gunship Tiger Fifty Seven Seven. Stand by for new orders."

"Ask and you shall receive," said Howton. "Got your ass covered back there, Doctor Death?"

"Wrapped in a pimp Cadillac, you limp-ass white boy. What's the poop?" sang out Doctor Death.

"No poop. We hang on to our Mystery Guest and wait for the sun to shine."

"I'm getting restless back here, boss. I ain't killed nothing all goddamn morning and I am getting a considerable mad on."

"How is the war going? Are we winning?" I asked Howton, although that was what I myself was here to find out and I knew Howton had no answers.

"War can't take you no place but cold and old. You ask me how the war's going, I'll tell you I miss the hell out of my wife and I don't think I'm ever going to be young again. You ought to be asking Doctor Death," suggested Howton. "If he don't exactly know the answer, he's sure-ass good at making up one that sounds good."

"Doctor Death?"

"Who that yammering in my ear?" said the big black with a wide grin splitting his face. "Is that the baby we want to throw out with the bathwater?"

"Affirmative."

"Welcome aboard, Chief. You out here trying to do to Vietnam what your folks done did to Custer?"

"Something like that," I said. "How do you think the war is going?"

"Just like a waitress with her legs crossed and her arms folded. The frigging service here is terrible."

Howton smiled and jerked his thumb back at Doctor Death. "His name is actually Jackson Jackson, but Doctor Death suits him better. Unwise to try to unconnect him with his own label. Ain't saying he's mean, but his pockets are full of teeth donated by second place in arguments with him."

"Sounds mean," I said. I spoke into the headset. "Once a tribesman, Elk Shoulder, fought many enemies single-handed, as many as the bar could hold, I guess. He said he didn't like the damn white man music on the jukebox. Survived the fight without a scratch. He grabbed some guy's head, tore the legs off a bar stool, and beat on his head right along with the music, singing he don't know exactly what because he don't speak any English, but no matter 'cause he's got the rhythm down, that's for sure. And he walked off, where somebody else would have died. If you get the rhythm, it is said you can walk off. When you talk, I hear the same rhythm."

"That's me to a T. I am the King of Walking It Off," said Doctor Death. "I am so goddamn mean I am going to survive Vietnam. Man, you can't get no meaner than that."

Another chopper, a gunship, joined us on the helipad.

It discharged several men, two guns at ready, obviously guards, with a prisoner between them, and a man walking like an architect's idea of what a human would walk like if he were a high-rise.

"Big lettuce coming, massa," said Doctor Death. "Look like to me we done getting the head dude."

Howton snapped a crisp salute, his face blanking, becoming an expressionless mask. Even Doctor Death stopped smiling as General W. approached the craft.

The general spotted me, smiled warily and gave a brisk salute. I did not return it. He did not seem surprised by my lapse.

"You're Lieutenant Lookspeaker? You know who I am. Let me make this perfectly clear. I have no part of this project other than arranging its final implementation. I decidedly do not approve of your mission. Is that understood, soldier?" The general's face was red, his voice clipped mean like overmown grass.

"I understand, General."

"I don't think you do," snapped the general. "In any case, I am delivering for interrogation purposes, or rather for what I assume is interrogation purposes, the highest-ranking VC prisoner we've got. His name and rank is—"

"I don't need to know that."

"Will you need an interpreter?" asked the general. "It wasn't mentioned but I have prepared for the contingency."

"That won't be necessary."

"You speak Vietnamese then," said the general, looking surprised.

I shook my head no. "I'll find out what I want to know from him anyway. It doesn't matter if I can't understand his language. What's important is that I understand his dreams."

The general contained his fury but it was an effort.

Through clenched teeth, he said, "I have been instructed to make a chopper and crew available to you with unrestricted flight plans. I have also been instructed to provide you with anything, in the way of hardware, ordnance or men, to accomplish your mission."

"I have what I need. Unhandcuff the prisoner and we'll be off."

"Would it be out of line to ask where the hell you intend to go?"

"Probably not, but I don't know where we're going, so I can't tell you."

The general looked troubled. "Is it true, the rumors, what they say about you?"

I smiled. "I don't know what you're talking about, sir." I gave him a sloppily executed salute, my hand coming off my nose like an inept karate chop.

That seemed to be the final straw for the general. He barked commands at the guards, who unhandcuffed the prisoner and helped him up into the bay door of the chopper.

The general spun on his heel and marched stiffly off like a man going to his own execution.

Howton shook his head. "Bloody m. f-ing Christ! I don't know what you're up to, Chief, but anyone who can twist the Old Man's mammaries in the wringer has sure got my vote."

Doctor Death regarded the prisoner balefully. "Hey, do I got to baby-sit and protect our ass, too?"

Howton turned to me. "He ought to be tied up. You can't trust the bastards any farther than you can . . ."

"No need." I smiled at the prisoner. He seemed relaxed and cheerful. Undoubtedly, he already sensed that I would be setting him free. I send a lot when I begin receiving.

"He'll be OK. Give him a cigarette, if you have any," I said into the headset.

Doctor Death looked disgusted at the idea of sharing with the prisoner. "Man, I got bullets extra I could spare, but smokes, you must be funning!"

"Where to?" asked Howton, cranking the chopper up for flight.

"North, I think. For a while anyway. I'll tell you when to change direction as soon as I know."

"Are we heading for some real deep stuff? I mean, give me some kind of idea what to expect. North to what, over what?"

"Don't expect anything," I said. "That's probably the best way. I'd like to fly slow and fairly low. We'll be in the mountains mostly, is my best guess."

"Guess!" Howton lifted us off. "It don't sound like you know what the hell you're doing! This ain't no place to be guessing about anything! Just thinking about it makes my BVDs want to seize up!

"You copying this, Doctor Death?" said Howton into the headset.

"Somebody better tell this dude that low and slow is full of lead and dead! Lordy, massa, this fool Indian keep pulling our tail with this kind of thing, I am going to frag his act right where it live."

"He ain't happy," said Howton as the chopper began flying over low-lying mountain ranges. "And I ain't getting ready to write you no love poems either. You're beginning to sound like a raffle ticket for buying the farm."

I pointed. "Go in that direction. Toward the highest mountain peak."

Howton looked at me like I was crazy. The chopper responded to his touch on the controls, tilting to go in the direction I had pointed.

"I think that mountain is where we're going," I said, not knowing it for sure until I had said it. Once spoken, it sounded strangely right.

From somewhere to the left of and a little behind the chopper, anti-aircraft guns began rattling at us.

Doctor Death leaned out the door, at the ready. He turned and looked back at us. "Unfriendlies, a day late and a dollar short."

In front of us, a jet dropped down at us seemingly from out of nowhere.

Howton grabbed the controls, ready to jerk us into an evasive pattern, expecting a missile launch.

"Relax," I said. "The sun is in front of us and a little to the right. If this were noon, we might be in a lot of trouble but it's late enough we . . ."

Howton knew then that I was crazy. I could see it in his face.

The jet roared down out of the sky, a missile was launched. It screamed by us, close but striking to the left and behind us.

The jet flipped over, pulling out of the dive, and put itself into a pattern for another pass.

"I'm going down," said Howton. "I haven't got enough go-juice to beat the . . ."

The next missile was launched. It followed the same pattern as the last missile, exploding harmlessly against the lower slopes of the mountain.

"They can only see our shadow," I said, looking back at the rising mushroom of smoke from the missile. "Trust me. They can't see us."

As if to further prove my point, the jet returned on a strafing run. It streaked down beside us and laid a perfectly executed fire pattern across our moving shadow.

Howton muttered something under his breath and made the sign of the cross. "I don't understand it. I must be stoned on my f-ing ass."

"There!" I said, pointing at the horizon. "You'll have to go up a couple thousand feet. Where we're going is just beyond that mountain peak. There should be a valley there."

"I don't see any mountain!" Howton had a haunted look on his face. "What goddamn mountain? All I see is jungle! Goddamn jungle!"

I spoke into the headset. "You see the mountain, Doctor Death?"

"You order me to see a mountain, I'll see a frigging mountain, but you ask me, I see only ugly goddamn jungle, is all." The big black had a firm grip on his machine gun, as if its proximity gave him security of some kind.

"Take my word for it, there's a mountain there. If your prisoner could speak English, he could tell you he sees it, too. He saw it first actually."

I didn't tell them that I saw only jungle, too, when I looked out the window of the cockpit. The eyes can lie, in a world of shadows.

When I looked into the Vietnamese prisoner's dreams, I saw the mountain. No jungle, just a single great mountain shining in the sun. I knew what I had come to find was on the mountain I could not see.

We gained altitude until I felt we must be well clear of the highest reach of the mountain peaks.

We spiraled in for a landing.

"Better slow your descent," I said. "And go a little to the left. There's a flat place where we can land just a little beyond the ridge."

"I don't know what you're smoking, Tonto," snapped Howton. "I don't see a ridge. I don't see anything except jungle."

I had my eyes closed, my eyes going inward. I could see the mountain as clear as I could see my hands.

"Just humor me," I said. "Make a descent slow and gradual. Just kind of drift down. I'll tell you when we're on the ground."

Howton complied with murder in his heart.

There was a soft thump and our descent halted.

"Hey, what was that?" said Howton. "We've stopped moving."

"I know it looks like the ground is still a long way down but we've actually landed. Turn the engine off. Once you step outside, everything should be all right."

Doctor Death leaned out the bay door, looking down. "Hey, Hownow, my underwear is seizing up on me back here! Tell me you ain't going to shut the engine off!"

I opened the door and jumped out of the chopper. Doctor Death shrieked. "Howton! The man done killed himself!"

As I stepped out, I saw only the ground thousands of feet below me, but once my feet hit, I saw the mountain.

Howton stared at me, his face showing a considerable strain.

"I'm standing on the mountain," I shouted over the roar of the blades. "Shut the engine off."

Howton shut it down.

Doctor Death stared down at the ground, a look of absolute terror on his face.

"Everybody out," I said as the whine of the blades subsided. "You can only see the mountain when you're on it."

The Vietnamese general smiled and walked calmly past Doctor Death. The black pivoted, brought his gun up to cover him. With a smile, the general stepped out of the bay door and dropped down.

He fell a few feet and stopped.

Doctor Death shook his head, rubbed his jaw once as if trying to erase the whole crazy thing, then said, "Ah, what the hell, you only live once."

He jumped out of the chopper.

He nearly dropped his weapon. "Christ on crutches! I'm on a goddamn mountain!"

Howton climbed out slowly, hesitated a second or two before putting his foot down on what seemed like air. He, too, saw the mountain. "I don't understand it. There's no mountain here! It's not on any of my maps! There's not supposed to be anything here but jungle and swamp! Where the hell are we?" said Howton. "If this mountain has never been mapped, somebody has really screwed the pooch! It doesn't make sense to me; somebody has to have seen it before! It's too big to damn well miss!"

"No American has ever been here before. We are the first and maybe the last," I said, reaching through the back door and dragging out the eagle cage.

"But what is this? How come we couldn't see it until we stepped out on it?" asked Howton.

"Vietnam is a land of shadows. America is fighting a war against something it cannot feel, cannot see or sense."

"What we doing here, Chief?" said Doctor Death. "This place gives me the shrieking freakings."

"I have been sent to find out if America can win this war. Now that I've found this mountain, I think I'll soon know the answer."

"That where the eagle comes in?" asked Doctor Death. "Everything is so messed up here, the craziest answer got to be the most logical one."

"Yes. That's why the eagle is here. That's why we're all here. We've come all this way just to play the ancient game of Cat and Eagle."

The VC general turned and spoke to me. I nodded and pointed up the slope of the mountain, then smiled at him.

"What did he say?" asked Howton. "I thought you didn't understand his lingo?"

"I don't know the words, but I understand the sense of it. We've got some climbing to do. The general has graciously agreed to lead the way."

"He'll lead us right into an ambush," snarled Doctor Death. "No way I'm going to follow him. I want him walking ahead of me but just so I can keep my gun aimed at his goddamm—"

"He is free to go at any time," I said. "And he knows that."

"Are you authorized to let him go?" asked Howton. "Or shouldn't I be asking?"

"I have no choice. This is a strange place we are in. You'll see what I mean. For one thing, I don't think your weapons will work here."

"Say what?" said Doctor Death. "What kind of craziness are you talking about, boy? If I aim at something, it's dead!"

"Not here. Hand me your weapon. I'll demonstrate."

"You find yourself your own weapon, boy. This one is done occupied."

Howton reached into his flak jacket and started to pull out a .45 pistol.

I waved the pistol away. "OK, if you don't believe me, try to shoot me."

Doctor Death looked at Howton. Howton shrugged.

"Just aim at me and fire."

Doctor Death just stared at me. I looked at Howton and nodded.

Howton took the pistol, extended it two-handed until it was pointed at my head. "You get what you ask for in this man's . . ." He pulled the trigger. Nothing happened.

Howton dropped the pistol. "OK, you've proved your point. Where do we go from here?"

"We leave the weapons behind. We've got a bit of a climb ahead of us. I don't know how far we've got to go or what's waiting for us when we get there. I don't think the general knows, either. He's never been here awake before. So most of what he knows of this place is only half remembered or very hazy."

"I don't go nowhere without my weapon," said Doctor Death.

"The eagle is our only weapon, and if you don't believe in the strength of the eagle's heart, this last part of the journey may not be for you. There is no dishonor in not going."

"Man, you have got to be kidding. You can't kill no VC with a frigging eagle! I don't want no part of this action!"

"Then stay with the chopper," I said. "You can stay, too, Howton, if you want to. There's really no need for you to go."

Howton scowled, straightened his shoulders and looked up at the ridge ahead of us. "I'm going to see what's on the other side."

I nodded approvingly. Howton was a brave man. But if I were going into combat, I would rather have had Doctor Death at my back. Howton would walk into the unknown, pretending not to be afraid. Only Doctor Death, who believed only in his weapons, had enough fear to be truly brave. He fought scared and therefore more truly alive than Howton, who tried to bury his fear.

He set off at a brisk pace until the going got rough.

"There should be a trail here somewhere, but the general doesn't remember where it is."

Howton looked uneasy. "Sounds weird, but since you mentioned it, I think the trail is to the left about a hundred feet. Don't ask me how I know, it just seemed to pop into my head."

I turned and walked in the direction Howton had indicated. I saw the trail.

"Glad you came along," I said. "This will save us hours."

The general walked up the trail ahead of us. He acted like a man in a dream, eyes nearly closed in sleep, stumbling like a robot up the path. He had the look of a sleepwalker.

The path came to a fork. The general stopped and looked back at us. He motioned first to the left and then pointed his finger at his chest. He pointed to the right fork, then signaled that we were to go in that direction.

I nodded. The general waved slowly as if we were already far away and then turned and stumbled off to the left.

"He's escaping!" said Howton. "And we just let him, right?"

"Yes. But it's more than that. Try to walk down the path he's taking."

Howton moved to the intersection of the two paths. He eyed me strangely for a few seconds then tried to follow the general. He seemed to freeze in midair.

"Just like the weapons, right?"

"And the general couldn't have gone down the path we're going to take. I knew something like this would happen. Didn't know how or in what way, but it's what I meant when I said we had no choice but to let him go."

"I think I can say, with a hundred-percent accuracy, that I am scared out of my freaking gourd!" said Howton. "I'm not that far away from the screaming—"

I interrupted. "I feel worse than you. If it helps any, you're going to come out of this alive. You'll make it back to the chopper and you'll make it back to base. So will Doctor Death." I didn't tell him that I would die here on this mountain even though I was as sure of it as I was of anything. It surprised me that Howton was admitting he was afraid. Maybe he had passed his limit.

We topped a rise and stood in a small clearing. Below us, we saw a valley, lush with vegetation. I knew we must be nearing the end of our journey. My arms were aching with the strain of carrying the heavy cage. I had a couple more scratches where the eagle had got at me again through the bars.

The trail led downward.

We began our descent.

I watched Howton now as much as I watched my footing on the path. My blindness was growing as his own vision grew.

He stopped suddenly, staring at something I could not see.

"What is it?" I asked, and stared in the direction Howton was looking. I saw nothing but trees and vegetation.

"I see people. At least, I think it's people. And a village, but it doesn't look like a Montagnard camp."

"I can't see it, but let's leave the path and walk toward the village," I said, and the Ancient of Lizards moved in the desert of my memory, seeking a distant sun.

"What do you mean you don't see it?"

"You knew where the trail was and I didn't, neither did the general. Now you see the village and I can't. Like I said, this is a strange place and things happen here I can't explain."

We left the path and moved farther down into the valley. It was a rough descent for a while and then suddenly it was much easier.

"We're on another path," said Howton. "It seems to lead directly into the center of the village. Did you see it?"

I shook my head no. My blindness was growing. I looked back the way we had come. The trail and the mountain behind me seemed to vanish in the distance. Perhaps I was near my own death now. I could not tell.

We walked on, Howton leading, me stumbling along in the growing dark behind him. Howton stopped.

"Where are we?"

Howton turned and looked at me. "Either I'm having the granddaddy of granddaddy hallucinations or we're standing in the center of a village and we're surrounded by the entire tribe, it looks like."

"What do they look like?"

"Like something out of a bad trip. Their eyes are strange. Like they are looking at things I can't see. They don't look like they ever laughed. This will really freak you, Chief. I think they got too many fingers on each hand. You suppose they are cannibals? I don't like the way they're looking at us."

"Describe how they are dressed," I said, cursing my blindness.

"In all the colors of the rainbow," said Howton, awed.

"Can you hear them speaking? If so, how does it sound?"

"It sounds like wild animals talking," said Howton. "You ask me, I'd say they are definitely hostile!"

"Look carefully. Are you sure they are not Montagnards?"

He shook his head. "They're like no Montagnards I ever saw. They're taller, and they've got—"

"I have to try to see them. I want you to close your eyes and keep them closed."

"You sure that's a good idea, Chief? They're brandishing weapons and they look downright hostile."

"They can't hurt you," I said and I closed my eyes.

When I was a young man climbing the lodge pole into manhood, I sought visions of power and wisdom. I chose the road of the shaman, and my vision ally was the spirit of a Great Snake. I called upon the Great Snake to make my eyes unblinking and terrible like his. I called upon him so that I might see into the shadows of this place that is the heart of Vietnam which no white man had ever seen before. If the Ancient of Lizards was my ally, far greater was my Nightfather, the Great Ancient of Snakes, whose tail was wrapped around the center of the earth. In him, terrible and grim, lie all the truths of man.

I felt the presence of the Great Snake, and the blindness, which was the blindness of the white man, dropped from me.

In my vision, I stood alone on the mountain. The white man with closed eyes was gone. Then my aloneness was pierced by the war cry of the people of Vietnam's hidden heart. They attacked. They were strong, clean-limbed people, tall and golden in color. They killed me and cut my head off.

My head was on a spear made of gold, carved in the shape of

an entwined snake. The eyes of the snake were red gems, gleaming in the hot sun.

My eyes were still open and I still saw. I saw what the white man could not see.

Beneath the shadows and smoke lived another Vietnam. These were the unseen ones, the ancestors of the people yet to be.

In the center of their village was a not alive, not dead statue of the Great Cat of Death. It was the one true symbol of this world the white man could not see.

This was a village that had been here since the beginning of beginnings and would exist long after the white man was gone.

An old man came and sat beside my disembodied head. "Why have you come so far to die?"

"I have come to play the game of Cat and Eagle," I said from my ghost mouth.

"No man has ever played it before. Already you are dead and have nothing left to win. Would you still play?"

"You know in your heart why I must play. Dead I may be, but I yet clearly see."

"If the eagle wins, I will give you back your life, your head back to its body. But know you that the Great Cat is strong and clever. He fights in his own land, where none but he is kin and king. Does your eagle see, heart true, so far from home, dead man, this is what I ask you?" said the old man.

"Only by playing the game will we know."

"Let it be so then," said the old man. He took the cage of the eagle and held it out in front of him at eye level, as if it weighed nothing. Carefully, he opened the cage door and reached in with one hand and took hold of the eagle. The great bird tried to attack him but the old man seemed made of granite, not even flinching as the bird tried to sink its talons in his arm.

The old one held the bird aloft, firmly holding it by the legs. "Great Bird, you see before you your enemy, the Great Cat. I make ready to send you to him."

My ghost eyes saw the living, not living statue of the Great Cat twist and arch its back, rising up off the great block of mountain stone. It snarled, its eyes coming open and seeing its enemy preparing to meet it in combat.

"Go, Eagle! May you fight well and find a good wind!" The old man released the bird.

The bird shot up like an arrow into the sky, thrusting up on wings of death. Beneath it, the Great Cat crouched, its eyes turned skyward, seeking the enemy.

The Great Eagle rose up so high it was almost invisible. Then it dived down, in its long, graceful killing swoop, claws flashing, eyes burning with great hunting wisdom.

The Great Cat seemed to stand helplessly in its path, making no move to avert the Great Eagle's killing plunge.

The Great Cat screamed. The Great Eagle struck, winged lightning falling upon its intended prey.

The Great Eagle's talons closed on air.

Unseen, the cat came up underneath him, and in one murderous lunge, seized the great bird and defeated him.

The Great Eagle's skull was crushed in the unseen jaws of the Great Cat of Death.

"The stranger is dead and the Great Cat has triumphed," said the old man. "So do the dreams of men die when they are not alive in the world they belong in. You have come from a great farness to see my people and our ways. Your people long ago walked in the same path as we once walked. The white man is not of your way or of ours. They come upon our path, but the way is forever barred to them. So it is with your people and ours."

I spoke from my dead mouth. "I knew that my bones would dwell among your people. The white men sent me to find out if they could win the war."

"They seek and we hide," said the old man. "So shall it always be. The white man cannot defeat what he cannot see, cannot conquer a land he cannot find. That is your answer."

"I wish to go home and be among my people."

"Leave your body with us and go back in the mind of the white man," said the old man. "We shall grind up your bones and flesh and eat of them, so then shall your ancestors join us in the flesh and blood of our children yet to be."

I closed my eyes for the last time. I had died.

Lieutenant Colonel J. N. Howton sat in the cockpit of his chopper. Doctor Death stared at the body of the Vietnamese general.

His gun was still smoking.

Howton turned in his seat, startled by the sudden burst of gunfire. "What happened?"

"I don't rightly know. One minute I'm watching his ass and the next minute he's charging down my gun trying to push me out the door. He just freaked out!"

"We'll probably get our noses ripped off for losing him," said Howton with a scowl.

"And Jesus, the bastard must have killed the eagle! I don't know how because I had my eye on him all the time, but this damn bird is sure dead. Ripped to shreds! How do you figure it, Hownow?" said Doctor Death.

A sudden burst of flak from the ground caused Howton to veer sharply to the right. "Big unfriendlies with nasty stuff!" said Howton. "We're going up and away."

He turned to me with an apologetic grin. "Sorry about your prisoner. Guess he did in your eagle, too. I said you can't trust the—"

He stopped talking when he realized I had been hit.

I could feel blood running down my neck. I didn't feel any pain, just a great coldness from my shoulders on down.

"Oh, Christ! Doctor Death, we got a casualty up here! The Chief picked up a package!"

"Head for home, Hownow! We got us a blown gig for damn sure!" cursed Doctor Death, leaning out the bay door, his heavy machine gun spitting angry death at the jungle below.

Howton increased the chopper's speed as he spun in a wide turn, heading back for base.

Howton spoke into the radio. "This is Nine Nine Four on the LOOKSEEK run. We've got one dead VC and Mystery Guest wounded. We must abort. Requesting medical assistance."

"How bad Mystery Guest?" I heard the radio immediately reply. It was the voice of General W. himself. I motioned weakly with my hand at Howton, but he didn't see me. I wanted to tell the general something but my mouth couldn't form the words.

"Very bad," said Howton, staring at me. "Head wounds at the base of the skull. Don't know if he'll make it."

"Get back as quick as you can," said the general. "And I'll want a full report of just how this thing got screwed up. You did your best, men, considering the assignment," said the general, signing off.

"I expected you to get your ears pasted back," said Doctor Death. "The Man sounds like he's glad the whole thing went into the toilet!"

I was beginning to lose consciousness. I knew I was dying. "Tell the general we can't . . ." I couldn't get the words out. Seemed so tired, so cold.

"Take it easy," said Howton. "We'll be home soon."

"No," I said and the pain began and almost obliterated me. "War . . . can't win . . . white men . . . in wrong Vietnam . . ."

I died in the cockpit of the UH-1D. At the moment of death, in the village on the mountain which the white man could not see, the women ground up my bones and flesh in a stone bowl.

The old man, the World Knower, came to sit beside the statue of the Great Death Cat. When the women had finished their task, they brought the stone bowl to him and he offered some of it to the Great Cat.

Then the people of the village came with bowls of food, and in each bowl, he put a small ancestral piece of me.

They ate of me and I became one with their children to be, one with the children that would live on in that world long after the white man was gone.

In a vision, in a rapidly moving helicopter, somewhere above a Vietnam the white man couldn't see, a Great Eagle died in the unsensed jaws of a Great Cat.

The Becalming of Wind River's Horse

Wind River died in a white man's prison in 1897. His wife died of starvation waiting to receive the bones of the man she had loved. His bones were lost in a mass grave.

She was buried somewhere, exactly where no one knew. It too had become no longer important.

Their only daughter lived outside Fort Kearny, drank a lot with the white soldiers and was dying slowly of bad whiskey and tuberculosis.

The only thing left of the old days was Wind River's war-horse. His daughter vaguely remembered she had the horse, watered it when she remembered. Mostly it was turned out to graze and she forgot it was around.

The horse had no name. He was simply Wind River's horse.

And he was dying.

He had fallen sick.

Because he had been a great war-horse, the remaining survivors of the tribe said it would be bad medicine to kill him, even though his hide would make fine leather and he would be very good in the eating pot.

But honor was honor. They would not kill him. They were hungry always, but they did not think bad thoughts about the horse or blame him for taking too long to die.

No one came to stroke his head or comb his long mane; no children leaned against his sides, dreaming of the days when they might sit astride a great wind with four legs.

Only the vultures, black and ugly creatures with dark hearts the color of their feathers, kept him company.

Sometimes the dogs of the village came to see him, dogs he had joined in great hunts long ago, but their visits brought no comfort to Wind River's horse.

The souls of dogs are ugly with too much contact with men.

Sick, alone, the horse lay on his side in the long grass.

Nostrils quivering, he sniffed the wind, sensing danger, and struggled painfully, stiffly to his feet.

Death was in the wind. The old war-horse felt it burning against his bones. He whinnied in terror, eyes dilated, nostrils flaring.

He feared everything now. Night most of all, because death was always so strong then, and the wind, the cruel wind which seemed ever to have the smell of decay tainting it with its sweet, acrid sting.

The old horse raised his head, trying to read the wind, and turned to run from death.

Neighing long and shrilly, he tried to run.

At his back, from the hills beyond the village, came a rustling, and a humming and a scurrying.

A black loathsome thing, the smell of just such a thing as that, came to the old horse clearly on the wind.

The horse bolted, the once proud war-horse legs churning as the old horse ran to outrace death.

Now Wind River's horse thundered across the land like a bow-driven arrow, flashing in the last rays of the setting sun.

The sun was in front of him, blinding him, outrunning him, seeming to be uncatchable life lived forever, and the old horse stumbled and he nearly fell. His pace faltered and his feet carried him off the great trail of war.

Now the sun was behind him and the old horse seemed to be racing headlong to meet death.

In blind panic, the horse turned and ran again for the sun.

To stop was to die.

But to run farther was to collapse from pain.

The old horse slowed to a walk. Panic and a fear as cold as a grave urged him madly to run, but his tired old body was unable to obey. He stood motionless, a great stunned, half-blinded thing.

Wind River's horse lowered his head and little by little, the fear subsided. The old horse came to himself again in the memories of the great hunts, the swift runs across the long grass in the full-legged glory of his youth. He remembered the stirring touch and warm presence of other young horses and the blinding heat of mating and fierce desire. He remembered the man who had ridden him, whose soul had been a part of his, whose triumph in life had been linked to his own. The good drove out the bad.

The sweet, rich taste of grass, the blue cool taste of running water. The good memories flooded in again and death seemed farther away.

Now the old horse felt strength returning to his scarred, time-ruined legs.

There awoke in him again a resistless desire to run. To thunder across the great fields of grass, forever chasing the sun. And also a desire to be one again with the man who had once ridden him in their shared glory. The horse seemed to know purpose now, seemed to understand that he must find Wind River once again so that together they could ride out the approaching storm.

Though he could barely stand on his own legs, though every step caused unbearable pain, the old horse began to run.

If the man would come just once again and sit astride his back or smooth his coat with one kind caress, gladly then he would lie down and die.

But dying alone under a sky filled with black birds of death was too horrible.

Blood spattered the ground, exhaled from his lungs in a red spray. His heart beat like a river rising against a dam.

On he ran, toward the dwelling of the man.

Not to die alone.

Neighing piteously, the old horse stumbled into the village, seeking the lodge of the man.

But a fence, built by the white men, barred his way. He pushed against the fence, but the rails were strong and did not give.

In despair, he tried to bite the rails of the fence but succeeded only in tearing his mouth.

He tried to rear up, to climb the fence, but his rear legs would not support him and he fell heavily against the fence. He leaned there, unable to go any farther, out of breath.

The old horse's eyes swept across the village eagerly, seeking the man, but the village seemed deserted, dying as he himself was dying.

The man wasn't here.

Somehow the dying horse knew it.

But where could he be?

Wind River's horse shivered. His eyes rolled and his old body shook like a leaf in the wind.

Each breath was like a knife scraping against his bones. His head sank until the damp grass touched his chin.

A great thirst came over him then and he wanted to lie down in water, to drink a river of it through his skin.

A vulture landed on the fence with a sudden flap of wings.

Wind River's horse found new strength in renewed terror.

He backed away from the fence, staggering onward toward the tall-spear rows of corn in the village garden.

The grass, which had always been life to him, seemed now like the long green fingers of death, catching at his hooves, trying to pull him down to earth.

Bushes seemed thick and unyielding, threatening to knock his legs out from under him.

All of the things of earth seemed to reach for his legs, to pull him eagerly down.

The soul of the old horse fell deeper into despair. He staggered blindly on. The vultures flew silently behind him, keeping him in sight, coming closer and closer, sometimes landing just behind him, sometimes just ahead of him.

His rear legs stiffened and began to drag behind him. Finally they failed him altogether, and he toppled sideways to the ground. The old horse thrashed on the ground, desperately trying to get back up.

The horse made it up off his side, rolled at last to a sitting position, his useless legs sprawled out under him like broken tree limbs.

The vultures flew down from the trees and hopped along the ground, coming closer and closer.

The long rows of corn bent in the wind and saw Wind River's horse with its many yellow eyes.

The old horse whinnied.

Still closer came the vultures, sharpening their claws against the hard ground.

Some flew overhead, circling nearer, almost touching the old horse's head.

Wind River's horse saw their dead eyes and sharp curved beaks.

He struggled to rise but his legs would not obey.

He tried to push his hooves against the ground and dreamed he was up again, the man on his back, racing across the long grass with one great shared wild heart, man and horse, riding the long back of the big wind.

Somewhere, a pile of bones stirred in the ground, shaking the tumbled bones of the many bodies buried there.

A great wind seemed to go down through the earth, down deep enough to touch and move the old bones of the dead. Wind River's horse neighed savagely and snapped his teeth at oncoming death, at the ever nearing vultures.

The wind shook the bones of the dead. Wind River heard his old war-horse, and as the spirit of one called to the other, he tried to rise above the ground.

But the weight of all the many dead weighed him down.

Wind River's heart wanted to beat again but there was too much death. His bones stirred, danced and ached to join up again but the other men's bones sent coldness and blackness and a despair so deep that it ate the wind that stirred the bones. And then Wind River's bones were still and would move no more forever.

Wind River's horse felt the last wind leave his mouth then. In that instant, he knew the man was dead and gone.

And then the old horse left the warpath. His hooves fell off into nothingness.

The green eyes of the grass stared in the horse's staring eyes.

The trees of night approached Wind River's horse and reached out their sharp clawlike roots for him.

The vultures came.

The black nameless things that hum and whisper and scurry began to crawl across the old horse's body.

The soul of the old horse rose up like smoke into the sky. On flashing hooves, it raced on a burning wind, seeking the man that had once shared that same great burning wind.

But the wind blew cold and from another direction now.

It came not from the great forest beyond the trees of night but from the spreading forests of tall buildings that house the white man.

It was a different wind and it had the smells of another world in it.

The soul of Wind River's horse grew cold. Its legs stiffened and its mane flattened against its side as the wind subsided.

Like a leaf, the soul of the old horse fell out of the wind.

And grew cold, and ceased to be.

And was seen no more.

When Death Catcher Paints the Wind

The bus pulled up to the reservation gate and the passengers disembarked. Only a few people got off.

There was a family of Japanese tourists, with the inevitable camera strapped around each neck. And there was me, a vast empty thing heading for a greater emptiness.

There was a hotel near the trading post where tourists and the professionally curious about Indians stayed. The bus passengers were bound for the hotel.

I was coming home to the reservation after two years in prison for stealing a car. Of the two hells, only the reservation was the one I called home.

On the bus I sat next to an old man and his daughter. The old man was a retired college professor, fairly old, nearing seventy summers. The girl herself was deathly pale, much too pale even for a white girl.

I wasn't much interested in them, but you can't help overhearing things on a long, hot bus ride. A bus is like a prison on wheels, there is no privacy and it travels, while you can't.

It seems the girl was going with her father to meet her husband-to-be, somebody from our tribe, Jim Longfeather, a man I never cared much to know.

His father had married into oil money and sent his son back East to some fancy white man's college.

The Longfeathers and I don't exactly move in the same path.

I also gathered that the girl had come out to the desert for her health. She coughed all the time, a dry hacking cough that sounded like the death rattle of a hand-tamed fawn.

I forgot about the white people when I got off the bus. My clan mother was there to meet me and my uncles from my father's side. They greeted me in the traditional way.

I walked home with them in the too-well-remembered heat

and dust, glad to shake the walls of prison off me forever. I hoped it was forever but there is no telling. I had had enough of the white man's prison. I would die first before I would ever go back there. Knowing my luck, it loomed as a possibility.

After supper, I went to my uncle Stormbringer's place to look at a new roan he'd bought and of which he was justly proud.

As I was walking down the arroyo where the old ones say the spirits dance, I met Jim Longfeather and the white girl walking toward me.

The girl was leaning heavily on his arm as they walked, heavily enough for me to see that she was pretty weak with whatever sickness she was struggling against. They nodded a greeting as I walked past. I asked Jim Longfeather in our language how his bones were.

"I'm sorry. I'm afraid I don't speak the language but nice to meet you." He stuck his hand out for a handshake. It was easy not to take it.

I went on past them. It figured, him not knowing the language. Having money can be a language all of its own. He was dressed like a city Indian too, clothes I don't know how to describe but you see them in those Sears and Roebuck catalogs, fancy-collared shirts and pants with some white man's name on the butt end of them.

I had had enough of white people to last me almost forever. I considered them both white. She was born to it and he had studied to become it. I did not want to think about them and dismissed them from my mind and went on about my business.

I forgot about them until the next morning, when dawn was just coming up and the sun was looking mean like it can look when you've drank a little too much. I ran into them again.

The night before my uncle Stormbringer and I had gone into the pueblo, to drink some of the ceremonial six-pack liquid. About the last thing I remembered was crawling out of Two Racer's back door to find something breathable. The night danced with fire, a remembered fire that was not my own, fire that came in bottles and made the head burn and ache with forgetting.

The white girl and Longfeather were sitting there, big as life, wrapped in a heavy Navaho blanket, watching the sun come up.

Now in the back of my mind, which had been scorched in a fire, was the idea that I might throw up a hugeness, something like the last two years of prison food in one big sprawl. Now here these two were messing up my big moment.

"Hey," I said—not much of an opening but then I was kind of dizzy.

"Oh, didn't know you were there," said Longfeather. "Hey, you speak English!"

"Grunt it is more like it," I said sourly. "What are you two doing out here anyway?"

"Waiting for Death Catcher to come. Do you know him?"

I did but I didn't talk about it. He was a brujo and a bad one or so the old people said. He had black gifts and saw things in the wind best left unseen, so it was said.

"What do you expect from him?"

"He promised to do a sand painting for her, something special for her, something he only does for a few people. Quite an honor, don't you think?"

I didn't say anything about the suspicion that grew suddenly in me but he had made me curious. "Why did he choose to do that?"

"Possibly out of respect for my late father. They were clansmen and related, by marriage if not by blood," said Longfeather. He even talked like a white man.

I stared out across the desert and the feeling of sickness began to pass. I thought, as the cool morning air passed in and out of my body, that I might yet live to see the day. I reserved that judgment about everyone else.

"You know much about Death Catcher? What they say he does?"

"Just that it's supposed to be special."

"Yeah, I've heard that too," I said but didn't speak of the other things I had been told, the dark things.

I heard something and turned to look over my shoulder. The air was clear as a diamond, and my Indian heart seemed to soar on the wind as I looked on the desert again.

The desert was as white as an owl's belly. Off in the distance, at the bottom of Black Mesa, I saw the lonely figure of Death Catcher, with a woven sack of clay jars on his back. He was a long way off, almost an hour's walk from us. The old ones say he casts a vulture's shadow as he walks. Maybe they are right.

The three of us sat there in silence, staring at the rising of the sun on the desert.

It was peaceful, calm like the dark eye of a storm.

The only sound was an occasional rasping cough from the girl.

The desert has a kind of beauty that is not always there for one to see. It is like a mirage that vanishes without warning, becomes a dull, flat deadly hell with no place for man. There was no sense of that now on this morning. Today there was only great beauty, rare and fine.

I don't know what Longfeather and his white girlfriend saw on that morning when they looked at the desert or if they looked at anything else but themselves, which is a way white people have of seeing the world.

But when I looked at the desert, I saw the old dead sea shining like a glowing pool of turquoise. I saw the bones of long-dead beasts rise on dusty wings and bone-white legs and fly and race across the face of the desert's ancient heart. Dead snakes coiled in trees a thousand years dead, waiting for birds with wings of dust. And the living, those I saw too. Lizards stalked and stabbed their tiny prey, bloodless dusty insects with the taste of forever in them. Eagles mated in the air in graceful golden arcs, and the sand stirred gently in the wind that was the very wind of freedom and life. There was no prison here, just the aching beauty of far far away.

I turned to look at the white girl to see how she was taking the desert at dawn. How white people will react to things is not always easy to figure.

She was leaning heavily against Longfeather under the blanket. I sensed that she might fall over if he wasn't holding her up.

She was crying. Softly, but crying all the same. Her pale oval-shaped face looked pinched and she seemed sicker than she had been the day before.

"How do you feel?" he asked her, worry plain in his voice and face.

"Better," she said and I thought she was lying, probably more for his sake than her own.

"The air here, the doctor said it would help. It just has to, Amanda. You just have to get well," said Longfeather. "You'll see, a week will make a real difference!"

We sat in silence for a time. I was over being sick. Even thinking about dragging myself up and getting out of there. I was beginning to feel quite another call of nature besides tossing my piñon nuts.

But by then, Death Catcher was almost upon us, and my curiosity was aroused. I hoped his being there had some other meaning than some of the things I had heard about him.

Longfeather started to get up to greet him, even offering to shake hands. The old man ignored him completely.

Death Catcher unpacked his clay pots and began drawing a rectangle in the sand with a specially carved stick.

Longfeather tried speaking to him, but the old man still ignored him. Longfeather turned to me. "Does he speak English?"

I shook my head no. "I've never heard he could. What do you want me to tell him?"

"Just that I am honored by what he is about to do. And I very much want to thank him."

I told the old man in our language what Longfeather said. The old man stared at me with an irritated expression on his face. He spoke slowly. "Tell him to step away. His presence is not needed."

I translated his speech for Longfeather. Death Catcher had also said some fairly nasty things about Longfeather's ancestry which I didn't dare repeat.

When I was translating it for Longfeather, I think the old man knew I left it out. I wouldn't have been surprised if he spoke English better than me.

Longfeather looked to me for an explanation for why he had to move away while the old man worked. I just shrugged. "Who can say why?" I said. "He doesn't do things for reasons that can be easily explained. Best to humor him and move back until he finishes."

He nodded, and somewhat begrudgingly moved off about a hundred feet and sat down again. A lizard jumped out of a bush in front of him and I heard him yelp in surprise. It made me smile. I kind of regretted I hadn't told him the old man wanted him to sit naked on a cactus to complete the ritual, just to see if he was city-dumb enough to do it.

Death Catcher was old, how old nobody quite knew. His white hair was thick like a pony mane and his hands were rough and scarred and slightly crooked with his great age.

Still his hands moved with grace and ease as he patiently began the sand painting. He carefully measured out the first sand, red, and sprinkled it on the ground. Then black. I watched the pattern being drawn.

The first thing I noticed was that the colors were all being reversed and that he intended to leave out some of the symbols. That was proper for a sand painting that was being done for public exhibition, for white people.

Death Catcher was not working in the sacred forms. Also the old man followed a dark and very old style, said to be a long-ago gift of the nightlands.

He used colored sand, cornmeal, flower pollen and several mixtures of powdered roots and bark.

He held out his hand and talked to the girl.

She stared at him blankly. Her head had sunk back until she was almost lying flat on the ground. She turned her head slightly until she could see me.

"Excuse me, I don't know your name but could you tell me what he said?"

"He wants you to give him something."

"What?"

"I don't know. Something that . . ." I asked the old man a question, making sure I understood exactly what it was he wanted. "Oh." I nodded at the old man. "He says he wants a piece of white writing. He wants something with your name written on it."

The girl thrust her arm out from under the blanket, pushing her purse into view.

"Could you look in there for me? I feel real tired. There must be something in there with my name on it."

I didn't much want to do it, but I did. I rummaged around in her purse. I got her wallet out and found her driver's license. "Mind if I use this?"

"No," she said. "And thank you."

I stuffed the wallet back into her purse and handed the old man the plastic driver's license. It had her picture on it, as well as her name. It was an old photo and she looked younger and healthier in it, almost like a different person.

The old man took the card, looked at it and nodded that it was what he needed.

Death Catcher stuck one end of the card in the right-hand corner of the sand painting, filling in the corner block around it with black sand.

I have never seen a driver's license used in a sand painting like that before. I wondered if the old man was playing some kind of joke on them.

But the old man had much too evil a reputation to be one for jokes.

I watched the sand painting unfold. I knew it would take a long time until it was finished.

I got up to go. I had to get rid of some of last night's beer. I went around the side of Two Racer's house and relieved myself.

When I came out, I saw my uncle Stormbringer standing down by where Jim Longfeather was sitting. They were talking and Longfeather was pointing in Death Catcher's direction. I sensed that my uncle was saying something that would shake the air like a storm.

I walked down to where they stood because I sensed that something was wrong.

My uncle had a very strange look on his face, like a man who understands the taste of poison.

"I don't understand. What are you trying to say?" asked Longfeather, fear in his face and eyes.

My uncle had his eyes turned away. "I said Death Catcher is not his only name, just the name that is his when the black winds blow and give him power. When he paints sand paintings, they call him Death Catcher."

"So what?" said Longfeather. "So he has more than one name."

My uncle just shook his head sorrowfully. "My heart walks on the ground for you. You have been too long from the people or you would know. They call him Death Catcher because he only does sand paintings for the dead. As a person takes his name out of the world, on that day, Death Catcher makes a sand painting for them."

"Nobody is dead here," said Longfeather in confusion.

"He paints them just before the person dies. In all the years Death Catcher has walked the earth, he has never made a mistake. Never. When he sand-paints for someone, that person leaves the world in death," said Stormbringer and he was genuinely sorry when he said it.

Longfeather screamed. He pushed my uncle aside and bolted toward Death Catcher and the blanket-wrapped figure of his white girlfriend.

"No!" he shrieked, and he knocked the old man aside. The old man, frail with many winters in his bones, fell heavily on his back, a clay pot of corn pollen flying over his shoulder and smashing against a rock.

Death Catcher lay flat on his back, not hurt, his eyes closed.

I had run after Longfeather, hoping I could stop him, but a night of drinking doesn't make for a good runner the day after. He had me beat by at least ten steps.

He thundered through the sand painting, scuffing and kicking at the rainbow-colored pattern, scattering it to all four directions.

It was desecration.

I jumped on Longfeather and tried to knock him down, afraid he was going to try to hurt the old man. He bobbed his head and threw me off his back like a duck shaking off water.

I landed in the wreckage of the sand painting.

Longfeather ran to the girl. The figure beneath the blanket did not move.

He picked her up gently and I heard him say something to her but she was strangely silent.

I sat up slowly, stiffly. I had come down pretty hard and my neck hurt bad. It ached when I tried to turn it. I wanted to move over to the old man, to see if he was hurt. But my uncle was already there, helping the old man sit up.

As I struggled to get up, my hand closed on something hard and I looked down and saw the girl's plastic driver's license stuck in the black corner of the sand painting. It was the only part of the sand painting that had escaped destruction.

I picked it up and started to look at it.

The old man opened his mouth and laughed. It was a harsh sound, cold and evil, and it chilled my bones.

I turned to look at the old man.

His eyes shone in triumph, reminding me of the dead, black eyes of a vulture.

I wondered if the girl was all right. I looked down at the driver's license and knew suddenly how she was.

Her name was gone. The old picture of her, taken when she was younger and healthier, was now that of a Navaho blanket-wrapped skeleton, painted on the wind by the Death Catcher.

On a Journey with Cold Friends: Novella

CHAPTER ONE

The shaman sat on the hard dirt floor of the ruined pueblo waiting for the rat of death.

The wound in his side was fire and ice. Fire that burned his flesh with the pain of it and ice that crept toward his heart as the blood oozed from the wound.

The soft keening of his death chant awoke the ancient rat.

Yasheya lay back against the crumbling wall, the strength of his days like sand washing away in a storm-burdened stream.

"Hola! Friend rat, picker of bones!" he cried, his eyes staring into the dark.

The rat, the long swift gray thing that stirred in the ancient walls, lifted its head, harkening to the old man's invocation.

Yasheya dipped a finger in the pool of blood at his feet. He held it up to his lips and blew gently on it, as if sending the red-blood rich scent of it through the ruins.

"Smell it, bonepicker. Arise and come to me. An invitation to a feast."

The rat arose from the gray dust and broken bones of its centuries-old nest. Its eyes burned in the dark with the power of old forgotten dreams, with the dark force of a thousand thousand moonless nights.

It moved quickly now, the old hunger and lust burning its blood. The rat came swiftly down the long tunnel, its dry claws rasping against the hard dirt floor.

The blood dripped down Yasheya's arm. The hand that held the wound trembled as if each step of the rat shook the floor like a time of thunder moving earth.

"I hear you, ancient enemy. Are your teeth still sharp and

wicked? Are your claws strong enough to tear my wind-and-age-hardened old flesh? I wish to see you, bone stripper! I call your name!"

As the rat passed down through the burial rooms, it tarried at the entrance to each grave as if tasting in memory the feast it had once had.

Yasheya gathered his failing strengths and final magics for the last battle.

The ancient face of rat enemy rose out of the dust at his feet.

Yasheya smiled and a spider crawled out of his mouth, a gray thing of ash and silken intent, a spider from the burning days, alive with ancient hatred.

Wary, the rat being moved back to a dark corner of the room.

"Who disturbs me in my dwelling?"

"I am Yasheya, once of this pueblo in the days of my younger being. I am Yasheya, the life taker and the stealer of men's faces," said the old man and his eyes blazed with sudden fire.

"You are only flesh and a taste I will soon have," said the rat thing, and his eyes opened and shut with quickening delight. The hunger began deep in his too-long-empty belly, made his whole body quiver with ancient, never ending blood lust.

"You have awakened my hunger. I will dance in your skull and eat the pretty memories."

Yasheya laughed. "Little brother of night, I will wear your blood-soaked fur for a death robe so that those in the spirit world will know my power."

The rat moved closer, tantalized by the feast. His teeth were long and wicked and yellowed with centuries of such feastings in the dark.

The spider scuttled across the floor, an eyeless, hungry sting, a shadow stalking a shadow.

Rat being eyed the spider calmly. "I do not kill easy," said the rat. "I have necklaces, pretty necklaces of human teeth."

"I do not die easy," said Yasheya.

The spider danced in a circle around rat enemy. Rat hissed, and hot sparks, vivid intervals of fire and death, raced across the dusty floor.

Hit in the fiery burst, the spider glowed red, fire-bright. The force pushed the spider back but seemed not to hurt him. If anything, spider was fire-born, and weird life pulsed even more strongly in him.

The spider screamed and danced and poised itself on the edge of stinging death.

"Tell me how it is that you come to me, old man. Knowing where the bones grazed in life, makes the meal all the sweeter."

The old man licked his lips. His tongue was heavy and swollen with the birth of the spider. The words did not come easily, but come they must, for it was part of his power and his enemy must know their sting.

"In the long grass days of youth, in this pueblo of now vanished glory, I was the chosen one. Here, like a tree from the center of the earth whose branches carry the sky, I was once master of the world."

The rat being laughed. It was a sound like knife scraping bone. "Boast not, old man. Youth does not last. Only appetite, only hunger, my hunger, that is all that lasts."

"So you say, but the stars fell from the sky and danced for me and the wind of life was ever at my back. The powers of all old and terrible things, the life taste of unseen killers of night, all mine for the asking in the below world of men."

"You think much of yourself, old man. What was, is nothing. Now you are only that upon which I will feed. A taste of bone and old withered flesh."

The spider leaped at the rat like a spark shot from a greenwood fire.

The rat caught it in its claws. Its hot tongue darted, stabbed and impaled the spider, pinning it to the floor; its sting and death drowned in the ancient taste of graveyard dust.

It burned and shriveled and melted on the ancient floor and the old man cried out as it and that part of him that the spider had come from, died.

The rat pulled the legs off and crushed the body in its yellow teeth and then spat it out, a misshapen clump of poisoned ash, the fire of old, forever dimmed.

"I would have destroyed you then," said Yasheya. "But I see you have forgotten nothing, that the simple tricks are still beyond you."

"It is useless to even try. Your bones are mine to pick, I only await the telling of your last tale, that last little bit of history that brings you to me."

The old man stared into the dark, seeing things beyond the ruined room, things of uncertain fire and misplaced feelings.

The rat crept across the floor, his ancient teeth longing for the pink temptation of the old man's throat. And as he moved slowly in the last darkness of Yasheya, the old man spoke.

"I, Yasheya, not born of men, son of rain and fire, once found in the depths of woman, brightly lighted riverbanks, where cries of joy shot forth. I have not always said yes to woman. Yes . . . yes to her glory and her burning desire to be the highest bird perched on the naked shoulder of night.

"And in this, I have found my life and lost it as well. I am here, bonepicker, the last man alive on earth, because although darkly powerful, and in that way beyond the common needs of man, I am not entirely without the spirit of man."

The rat moved in the darkness.

"I have expressed much tenderness, for one who might have been a dark spirit with mastery over life and death. I, Yasheya, inheritor of a killing storm, instead kept my black heart carefully even and small. I have lowered my intent red shaman's eyes beneath the inescapable stars."

"Foolish man," said the rat. "Power bridled is no power at all. Only hunger survives."

"I had power, rat enemy, and yet have it still, as you shall know when your lifeless body is before me, but power was not the one great answer I sought. Seeing the easy ruin of human life about me, seeing the useless charms they used to deflect me in my strength, then I, Yasheya, in those moments when not even still waters dared reflect me, even I wished, as the dark night was in me, wished for the pale view of morning that has been the eternal promise of all women born."

The rat stopped moving, its feet in the red pool of the old man's blood. It hesitated, fascinated by the old man's words, rapt, but ever ready for some final trick, for some hidden treachery.

Outside the ruined pueblo, the air itself burned with the final darkness of mankind.

"I never trusted men who sought themselves in women. They

are capable of anything. I should kill you now, old man, your history does not please me." The hunger was strong in him, impatient and hard to stay.

"It is life that displeases you, friend rat. And women are part of that mystery, to be in love and forever die to be reborn." The old man felt dizzy, not from the wound, but from the overpowering memory that surged within him.

The road became an old road he once walked in life, a window to his past, and hunter and hunted fled the ruined pueblo, helpless in the grip of the history, the coming from what had brought them both into final darkness.

And the old man became young again and the rat traveled on his shoulder, ancient teeth brushing the soft flesh of his neck.

CHAPTER TWO

Yasheya rode West into the night.

His back was straight and strong and his body young and alive with green spring. He and the horse were of the same strength, the same burning desires and sense of freedom.

Yasheya topped a bluff, pulled the horse in and looked down on the village of the enemies of his people. War-proud, he cast insults down upon the people below. None were there to hear him.

The village lay in ruins, lodges burned and burning, smoldering ash heaps littered with the dead. Yasheya cried out in dismay. He kicked the horse into a gallop and went plunging down the steep hillside, into the burned village.

One wished one's enemies ill, but not total destruction. Yasheya dismounted in the center of what had once been the home of a proud people, enemies, true, but brave and worthy enemies.

He stood silent and disbelieving and surveyed the tragedy. Men, women and children lay scattered around him in various attitudes of death.

A great death had stalked here, sudden unforgiving death, and Yasheya did not understand.

His own tribe had never made war on women and children. From that, he knew the killers were not of his kind.

A small girl in white buckskin lay half in and half out of the ruined lodge of Sakokimis, the chief. Her hair had burned away, and under her feet lay the broken water bowl she had been carrying when death struck.

The wind came down from the high bluff, pushing the smoke and dust away.

No one had survived. Everywhere Yasheya looked, was death. Horses and dogs lay scattered amid the other bodies. Great wounds were there in the still bodies on the ground but his keen eyes saw neither arrow nor spear.

What had befallen these people, what special curse of the spirits had visited this place, Yasheya did not know.

He turned and looked into the wind as if expecting to find an answer there, but it was just a wind blowing across the lonely grave of a people.

Then, on the wind, he thought he heard a cry, a strange ululation, and his hand touched his weapons and a sense of unease grew in him.

What spirit had visited this place? Could it still be near? Yasheya moved himself toward an answer.

Arrogant in his own power, his own sense of himself, Yasheya strode forth to face this evil. He wanted to test himself against it with the things in him that set him apart from other men. For Yasheya had great and dark and unspeakable things that were a constant wind at his back.

He let the horse go free as he strode in the direction of the sound. He heard it again. Strange and high-pitched, like some animal caught in a trap, like something pent up that should never be caged.

The sound came from behind huge boulders that littered the bottom of an arroyo.

Yasheya unleashed his medicine stick, muttering the words of power that made it dance with strange seethings. His weapons, forged in anger from the great stone bones of the old lizard people, were in his hand.

He moved like a ghost, like the shadow of a snake. His feet were deer-sure as he stepped through the broken boulders and rocks.

Now the sounds were clearer, coming from just ahead, around that last big boulder.

Unseen, unsensed, a gray rat thing swayed on his shoulder, like an obscene second head.

Yasheya sprang out from behind the boulder, to face what he knew not.

His weapons flashed and almost struck home but at the last second he stayed his hand. For it was only a woman, bruised and blackened with smoke. A woman heavy with child, in much pain and helpless before him, or so he thought.

"Why stay your hand? Kill me and kill two with one blow," said the woman, staring at him without fear. She was past fear now. She had seen too much, suffered too much to still fear death.

"Who are you? What happened to your people?"

She held her swollen belly and did not speak. He seized her arm roughly in the manner of a man forcing his will upon an enemy.

"Answer me!"

"I am a mother-to-be," she said. "Why hurt me again? Just kill me and end my pain."

"I have no cause to kill you."

The woman looked up into his eyes, saw things that danced behind them and looked away. "I fear you now. Your eyes are like shadows cast by birds."

"Enough of this. Answer me, woman." Yasheya set his medicine stick on the ground and slung his old bone weapons back on his belt.

"I am Minokos, the woman of Satay, now dead, as dead are my children, Miskos and Kukoskatta, as dead are all my people."

"What tragedy befell your people? What spirit or enemy descended upon your village?"

"Strange men from the East. White in skin, with hair of many colors, strangers in our land, perhaps not human, demons with long black sticks that spat fire and death. With fire and treachery, they fell upon us, and we were like the soft grass melting in a prairie fire."

"I would wish to see these men or demons." Yasheya looked to the East. "I have heard of these beings. It is said they were the first people of the horse. That they live in great numbers in lands far away, as many faces in the world as blades of grass, and all white as death. Tales were often told of these strange beings but never have I heard of them, in our land."

The woman cried out in pain. Her body heaved and buckled with the contractions of labor.

Tears welled from her eyes. "My child comes now, comes early, much too early. Leave me here. I would be alone."

Yasheya looked at her for the first time as a woman, not seeing the enemy. She was thin for one big with child. And young, younger than he had first thought. No more than sixteen snows, much too young to have lost the will to live.

Her face was blackened with smoke, her hair singed and curled by flame. Even under all that, she had a certain quiet beauty that might have touched the heart of a man, if he were not a man such as Yasheya.

She moved her head and Yasheya saw a cut on her forehead above her left eye. She rolled over on her side, swaying with the pain of the first contractions. Then he saw that her shoulder was wet with blood, that there were two ugly wounds there, where something had passed into the flesh and gone completely through.

Despite himself, Yasheya felt feelings he thought dead arise in him.

He who had no need for human companionship, suddenly found things in her face, etched with pain and grief, that he could not understand.

"I will help you."

"You are the enemy."

"Even enemies, I will help you."

"Go away. I don't need you."

"Your child needs me. You are hurt and have no women to help you. You have lost much blood. You will need an enemy's help."

But the old ways were strong within her.

"These are woman things. Go away. It is not right."

"To die being born is not right either." Yasheya bent beside her, taking her up in his strong arms, finding the close contact, the smell of her, disturbingly meaningful, feeling a tide rising in him never before awakened.

"Relax, little mother. You are the last of your people and I will help keep you alive by bringing the new little one into the world. If you will not accept my help for yourself, think of your people, who will live on in your child, the last of you to walk this earth."

She screamed with pain, her hand tightening in his. She looked at him, with sudden trust, with the kind of surrender of which only women in the world of men are capable, and Yasheya, in that moment, lost himself within her beautiful eyes, lost himself in a way past all his understanding.

Lost to a power as great as all the dark things that danced within himself.

The wind blew ash and sparks into the air around them.

In that lonely place beside the big death, a child came into being.

And vanished like a spiderweb ruined by the wind.

Yasheya held the soft dead little thing in his arms and it became, in that instant, his heart.

And he knew a sorrow that was like a deep blue pool in the darkest of caverns, without light or sounds or depth. It was a wordless age-old pain, as old as the earth itself.

And the child woman wept and held out her arms for the burden she would gladly have borne and he handed it to her.

She put the dead little one to her breast and tried to make it suckle, for she was blind with love and want and the vast ache of the First Mother.

And in the most terrible moment, as the knowledge of what must be done scraped his skin like a fire-hardened stick, Yasheya came to her and stood above her, raw with the pain of what must be.

Tenderly but firmly, he took the dead child forcibly away from her, easing its dead cold mouth from her warm chest.

As gently as he could, he put it down upon the ground, away from her, onto the cold loveless ground, a great part of which it had now become, losing its humanness.

And she cursed him and raged against him, feeling one thing and striking out at another. And even with her fury, they shared the same broken heart.

And then as the day died, she slept, exhausted, in his arms, and the weight of her pulled him down forever to the earth.

In the midst of that dark night, among the ruins and death, he became her man.

In the morning, finding herself still alive, the woman became his in spirit but not yet in body. That would come in time, when the nights grew long and the memories of this time became changed and somehow different in her woman's heart.

The rat of death hissed in the dark, hissed in growing impatience.

Its lust for blood was a raging all-consuming darkness.

CHAPTER THREE

The rat was burning to know the savor of his feast to be.

But the light, the great golden light of what had been, the coming from, yet held back the darkness of the ancient enemy.

And the history unfolded, neither rat nor man could stop it.

It did not begin at the beginning and it did not end at the ending. It went in all directions, both backward and forward, and it circulated like blood in an undying heart, Yasheya's heart.

Now it was in a time and place far from here, and Yasheya was the newborn son of a very old woman.

The boy's father was not human.

He was a thunder and lightning man. He had great powers and could talk to the wind. Also, by bleeding, from his eyes, he could make rain.

The old woman gave birth to Yasheya in the month of the blood-red moon. Yasheya's birth was a cause for much wonder in the village, for his mother was long past her summer of youth and the frost of old age had already whitened her hair.

Her back was bent with a life already lived, crookedly reshaped for the burial rack, yet she became with child and it came forth.

The men and women of the village came to see the strange birth of this child. They looked at the baby and they shook their heads, for Yasheya was not as a child should be. He was smaller than a baby coyote, too small to live, so the wisdom of the tribe decreed it.

"He can never grow up to be a warrior," said the chief of the village. "Such a tiny baby cannot grow to strength. It will not live to see the first snow."

Yasheya's mother arose from her blanket with the last of her strength, for she was slowly dying and would not live to see the end of Yasheya's birthing day. The old woman looked upon those who had come to pity and she said, "You are fools. My child, Yasheya, so I name him, will be more than just a killer of men, more than a hunter of deer. He is a gift from the dark house of the wind, from the things that walk at night. He was given to me by the Night Father."

This made the chief angry.

"Who, then, is the father of this child?" asked the chief, and he moved back a step, sensing a demon-caused thing.

"None may say his name," said the old woman, and the pain made her face white and the door of the grave opened and the oncoming night raised its hand of welcome to her.

"I have winter in my eyes," said the old woman, and her head fell back against the buffalo robes of the birth bed. "I have seen visions. I have danced in the darkest of nights and became with child because I know another truth."

"An evil truth," said the chief. And the people muttered darkly in agreement. The chief was angry and fearful, for the old woman had plainly committed a terrible sacrilege and the night child was the result of it.

The people began to edge back, sensing an unseen horror.

The chief pronounced his judgment.

"This child must be destroyed, for we know not the father, and wish no nameless, creeping thing, growing among our own children, spreading some night poison of its own making."

"Leave him be!" screamed the old woman, her face contorted with pain. "In my visions, I have seen him stronger than all of you, neither good nor evil, but poised at the beginning of two roads. Down one road, lies darkness, on the other, the far-going days of our race. Someday, he may lead us down one of these great roads." There was hope in her face and fear and even some measure of peace, for she felt the burden leaving her in the quiet at the end of the road.

"He must be destroyed. It is my judgment and it shall be done."

The shaman, Heart Killer, came into the room then and looked into the face of things beyond his own great powers, and said nothing. The people turned to him for an answer, but his face held none.

"Heart Killer, I call on you to judge as I have judged. We must destroy this night-fathered child. Is this not right for the sake of our own children?" asked the chief of the shaman.

All of the people crowded close, staring at the small, innocent, defenseless baby.

Heart Killer, the shaman, a man of great power and evil strength, looked down and saw into the depths of the child's eyes and screamed. He dropped his great medicine shield and his medicine bundle and ran, ran as if a wolf tore at his legs, stripping them to the bone.

And the people were terrified of something they could not feel or see or sense.

It was a great mystery.

The old woman seemed to sink deeper into her birthing robes, the life fading and melting from her bones. She was now powerless to defend her newborn child.

A shadow appeared in the doorway of the lodge and the cold wind walked into the room and touched each being in the room with the sharpened spearpoint of winter.

The shadow became a man.

It was Yasheya's father. The man that had been a shadow entered the lodge.

"None of you will raise a hand to destroy this child. He is a hope of the world yet to be. My woman has spoken true," he said, and the thunder and lightning crashed outside the lodge as if the world itself was angry.

"Look upon my son. He is like no other human being in this world. Do you not see thunder and lightning in his eyes?" asked the shadow man.

In great fear, the people looked and saw as he saw, for Yasheya's eyes seemed to flash and flare with a great storm in them.

And so it was that Yasheya came into the world.

CHAPTER FOUR

And ancient rat, unseen, crouched in the birth bed robes, hissing in anger and unslaked hunger. His eyes saw the beginning of the feast yet to come, a small baby with many days yet to grow before it would come dancing into the rat's ruined pueblo at last.

Later that day, the old woman closed her eyes for the last time and the people burned the lodge around her, to chase the spirit of death away.

Shadow father stood and watched the burning. He held Yasheya in his arms.

In his way, he had loved the old woman very much.

He was a thunder and lightning man, a shadow being of great dark power, but his heart was as soft as fawn skin. The death of the woman made the human world empty for him.

He no longer had a home there.

In the middle of their human night, at a time when his physical being was strongest, the shadow man left the village, vanishing into the night with baby Yasheya in his arms.

He went high into the mountains beside the sea and there he raised Yasheya far from the others of his kind.

The shadow man loved his son so much that he wished to keep him by his side in the nonhuman world. In that place, he would fashion a great shaped, spirit being of his half-human son.

So the shadow man hoped it would be.

But first it was necessary for the little one to be fed. Without a mother, the baby would soon sicken and die.

He took Yasheya to a special place high in the mountains.

He placed the tiny baby on a rocky ledge and then went even higher into the mountains, to the heart of his great power, thunder and lightning.

He became a shadow again and asked the lightning to find a mother for Yasheya.

And the lightning went journeying across the sky and touched the heart of a wolf.

It touched the sadness in the heart of a mother wolf, for her newborn cubs were winter-dead and her den was empty.

The lightning came back to the old man, burning the sky with a sad story, and the old shadow man sought out the young she-wolf.

Softly, in the language of her kind, the shadow being called her.

The wolf shook with the sound of distant thunder and came slowly, fearfully, out of her den. Her fur was blue-gray and soft as summer sky. Her eyes were quick and golden and full of the longings she felt for her dead pups.

The wolf began running down the mountain, in a thunder-quickened dance, down toward the innocent, storm-eyed Yasheya, lying naked on a rocky ledge in the sun.

The wolf did not know what called her, but it was something that pulled the mother strings of her heart and she had to obey. She came upon the baby suddenly.

She growled, hackles rising at the smell of human in the air. That familiar, hated enemy smell. And she would have darted forward, to attack, to kill and rend with her strong teeth, but the dance inside her was so strange a dance that she could not move. Not in that way.

The sudden hatred of human enemy tried to grow but it was such a tiny thing, all arms and waving legs, and something in her made the strange enemy smell seem unimportant.

In the rocks far above, the old one watched her and smiled, for he well understood her strange, savage mother's heart.

Yasheya cried, milk-hungry.

It was an appeal as old as the singing sky, a thing that all mothers understand. To the she-wolf, human or not, it was the sound of a baby that wanted to be fed. She came closer now, standing over the tiny human baby. It had the milky smell of the newborn.

She whined and tenderly licked Yasheya's face. In the dance that moved her, this strange baby reminded her very much of her own now dead pups.

Had it been one of hers, strayed from her at the time of birthing, perhaps touched by humans, and only now, newly found again? It was a question a heart asks, when it knows an answer it wants to find.

The she-wolf ran her cold nose across the tiny baby face. The infant was delighted with the attention. His short clawless hands gripped her fur, clinging to it with surprising strength.

The old one danced softly in the wind, an offering to thunder and lightning.

The she-wolf whined, more lonely now than ever before. The wolf part of her wanted to abandon this strange baby, this thing with a smell of humans about it. But the old man touched her once more with a flash of heart-reaching lightning, with a roll of deep thunder, and the mother part of her rose up.

And the wolf part drowned in the sudden flash flood of a mother's love.

Gently with her teeth, so as not to hurt the young pup, she seized the child, holding him securely the way a mother cat carries her kittens.

She began the long climb back to her empty den.

Yasheya did not cry. He liked this sensation of being carried, rocking back and forth, and he cooed contentedly.

The she-wolf's mate came out of the den when she returned. He was larger than she and his coat was a proud silver-gray.

The she-wolf laid the baby down at his feet. The male wolf smelled Yasheya carefully. He growled, scenting the newly taken meat.

He drew his lips back, showing his killing teeth.

It still lived, the prey was not dead yet, and he lunged forward to bite and kill with one quick snap.

The she-wolf jumped at him.

The force of her sudden attack knocked him flat to the ground. She bit him sharply and cruelly on his face and neck. He whined in fear and outrage and retreated, his tail flattened against his body.

She picked up the baby again in her teeth and carried him inside the den.

The he-wolf whined outside the entrance of the den. He hated having this strange thing in his den but there was nothing he could do about it. If his mate had adopted him, then he would have to adopt him too.

In the den, the she-wolf was a force that must be obeyed. It was a wolf way, and all the things of time could not change it.

The mother wolf curled herself around the baby in one corner of the den. Her mate crept slowly into the den. She growled at him but he made no move to bite at the little one so she let him come close.

Fearful that she might strike, he inched forward until his head almost touched her. She stood still, watching to see how he would act.

The he-wolf nosed the baby cautiously. Yasheya responded by wriggling happily at his touch.

The he-wolf licked the tiny human face, accepting him in the den, pleasing his mate, and then turned and went out to hunt.

Gently, the she-wolf gathered the little one to her. The milk which she had for her dead pups was ready for him.

His small mouth opened and she pressed him to her side. He found the milk and the ache in the empty baby stomach and the ache in the empty heart of the mother wolf were filled then to trouble them no more.

The shadow man ended his lightning and thunder dance.

The education of Yasheya into some of the special secrets of the world had begun.

The wolves cared for Yasheya all that summer.

Summer turned to fall and Yasheya grew strong on wolf milk and tiny bits of fresh-killed meat.

The wolves kept him safe from the dangers of the wild places, sleeping close by him in the dark of the den, warming his furless body with their own heat.

Fall gave way to winter.

Day by day, Yasheya grew stronger. And more unlike any child that had ever walked the face of this world.

For as he grew, the wolves taught him their wisdom, their great secrets and strengths.

CHAPTER FIVE

And thus he lived for several years until one day, the thunder and lightning man returned.

The shadow man came in a lightning bolt, splitting the sky. He crashed to earth, light and shadow in his face, great fear in his heart.

The sudden appearance of shadow father frightened Yasheya and he bolted, wolf-quick, for the safety of the sheltering den.

The old man caught him as easily as the wind catches the petals of a flower.

Yasheya was strong and could run like a wolf overtaking dawn, but still he could not outrun the lightning of the old one.

The old one spoke to him in the language of the wolves, for it was the only language Yasheya knew.

"You do not know me, but I know you," said the old one. "I am your father."

There was no word for lies in the tongue of the wolf, for none in that language can be told. Yasheya snarled. He knew this human-seeming one was his father but it did not mean he had to like it.

"You will get used to me," said the shadow man. "In time, you may even learn to like me, or more, be a son to your strange father. It is time for you to leave this place and journey once again with me."

"I am happy here," said Yasheya, and struggled against the shadow man, trying to break free from the old one's grasp, but he could not break free.

"You have learned all you can learn from the wolves, now it is time to learn of the ways of your own kind. Those things and much more."

"But I am happy where I am," insisted Yasheya with a growl, a wolf who would not give up his bone.

"Still you must come with me."

Yasheya tried to bite the old one but the shadow man held him so tightly that he could not sink his strong white teeth in the flesh of the shadow man.

Yasheya whined.

His wild heart struggled to escape as the old one dragged him higher up the mountain but he was powerless in the strong grip of shadow father.

Already he missed the warm den, the soft fur of his wolf mother and the loving ways of the wolf people, for wolves love their children as much as any who walk the earth.

Yasheya and the old thunder and lightning man went far. They traveled through the day and well into the next night. When the sun began to walk across the next day, they were in a hot land beside the edge of the great sea.

It was here by the great water that the further education of Yasheya began. The old man taught him the ways of wind and thunder. He taught him the dances and the languages of the night people, the dawn bird, the hurtling hawk, the night-seeing owl and the coyote and deer people.

And he learned the many lying tongues of men and the strange commerce of their speech.

The wolf mother became a buried love as Yasheya became a brother to everything that flew or walked or ran or burrowed beneath the ground.

The seasons unfolded and Yasheya grew with them. There was something now of winter in the speed with which he moved across the ground. There was something of summer in his heart when he stared at the night and saw things.

Like the frost winds, he painted his face on the hidden ledges of the high places. He made his way deep inside the mountain through caves no human beings had ever seen or would ever see. He held converse with great blind fish and lizards, rulers of a darkness complete and age-old. He learned the secrets of hidden pools, the infamy and treacheries of medicine wrought in darkness. From the blind fish, he learned something of eternity.

From the eyeless lizards, pale, boneless-looking beings who seemed more like the obscene white fingers of exquisite corpses, he learned stealth and solitude.

He had eyes from the hawks and learned their ways of seeing when he held them in his hands. He ran on the legs of the deer. In time he became as cunning as night coyote and could move like the shadow of a falling star when he made medicine.

Listening, he could hear the grass growing at his feet.

One day shadow father made camp on a secluded ledge high in the mountains. He built a small fire of dry wood and they warmed themselves against the chill of night.

"Father," said Yasheya, speaking now in the language of men, which was the language of troubles. "I grow restless."

"It comes when it comes. I have been waiting for it. I have prepared you for it," said the shadow man.

"I don't know why I am restless."

The old one threw more wood upon the fire, sending red-hot sparks soaring into the chill night air.

"It is time for you to take your place among your own kind," said shadow father.

"Why?"

"Because you must. Soon you must. You cannot waste all the things I have taught you. I want you to take these gifts, these ways of understanding, back to the people of your mother. You have learned much of the world that few living men know. In the days that will come, your people will face threats to the life of their world. You, Yasheya, are a knower of a way of holding truth, a truth that someday may end this threat to the life of all. That is what your whole life has been shaped to do."

"But why am I restless? I have always been happy here. Why am I changing now? What is wrong with me? I feel changes inside me. My body is changing and I do not understand it."

The old one held out his hands to the warmth of the fire. "It is the circle of life. Your body is changing into a man body. It asks to go back to its people. That is why you are so restless."

"And if I choose not to go," said Yasheya, "if I choose to stay among the animal people that are my brothers, among my wild friends with whom I share the same wild heart, what then?"

"Then you will be living a lie. You will be only a living dead man in this world. You must always live the life of the being that you are. You must know in your heart what it is to be a human being. That is what you are. To not try to learn to be a human being and walk in wisdom, is to be blind and to always ride the wind."

"But I don't know that other world. The human world is strange to me."

"You will learn."

"Will you help me?"

The shadow man stared into the fire. There was fear in his face. "I will try. I must not fail in this. I am not of that world, but as much as I know of it, shall be yours. I have put the tongues of many men within you, so that you might speak to them. So we have passed many of our long nights together. But I have so little time. It may be too late. I hope it is not too late, for I have lived past my time of being already and the knife of winter is deep in my heart. I do not think I will walk out of this winter. You may have to walk alone. If that misfortune should happen, it will be your first lesson about being human."

"Is that the way of the human world?" asked Yasheya. "Are human beings alone?"

The old one turned from the fire, a smile of unknown things on his face. "If that is the way of the human world, you must find it out for yourself. Tomorrow at first sunlight, we shall start for the village of your people."

Shadow father lay down by the fire, pulling his heavy white buffalo robe over him. Yasheya, like a wolf, turned around three times before settling in comfortably to sleep.

The shadow man felt a pain in his chest, and he sat up suddenly, and the fear leaped up strong in him.

"Yasheya! Wake up!" cried the shadow man.

With a snarl, Yasheya leaped upright, animal-quick, sense reading the all-around world for danger.

"What is it, shadow father?" Yasheya's alert senses had detected no intruder or threatened danger. "Who attacks us?"

"Time," said the shadow man. "It is time which drills a fine arrow point from a heavy bow into my heart. Yasheya, I am afraid to sleep for fear I will not wake."

"You are a being of thunder and lightning. How can you die?"

"Every storm must pass," said the old shadow man.

"Summon the thunder and lightning, as you have so often done. They will keep you strong," said Yasheya.

"Something stronger calls me," said the old one. His hand reached out for the boy. He put the palm of his shadow hand on Yasheya's face.

"Feel the power, Yasheya."

Thunder crashed on the mountain. Lightning streaked the angry sky. The wind came roaring down at them from the house of the north and scattered the fire.

"Take it into your being, Yasheya! Surrender your heart to the great unliving storm! Let it be you!"

Yasheya's body stiffened. The shadow man's hand seemed to be living fire, burning into Yasheya's skull. His face contorted in pain, his mouth hung agape. He writhed like a wild creature trapped in a sudden brush fire.

He screamed once, like a soul in the land beyond earthlight's torment, in the thirteenth and final hell of man, and then the surging current of the sky river, the raging fire storm, lessened.

And found every storm's season of calm.

Yasheya plunged downward like a man fallen off a mountain. He spread his arms and was uplifted. He found himself adrift on a great wind, and became a shadow being riding the mighty fist of the great north wind. He released himself, let his mind and body join with the great unfolding.

Yasheya vanished from the mountain. He became a summer storm, riding the crooked back of the highest far mountains, casting thunder-driven lances of fire, bleeding from his shadow eyes, unburdening cascades of fireborn rain. He was a terrible blizzard, burying the great world in a frost-woven blanket of white. He was a tornado tearing up the human forest and all in its path. He was a sudden squall at sea, racing across the face of the water, making widows for the men gone to sea.

And he was a gentle rain on the long green hair of mother earth.

The old one lifted his hand away, the transformation almost complete.

A bolt of blue lightning, as bright as turquoise, arced between them, the final passage.

It passed from the old one's eyes, gone from him forever, into the eyes of Yasheya, and the giving forth and passing on, was ended.

"It is yours now, Yasheya. I am an empty husk," said the old one, and he seemed to wither and shrink in the night even as he spoke. His strength was like sand in the river.

"Listen, Yasheya. I must hurry now. Before I teach you the last magic, before I teach you how to summon this great power and how you must use it, before this, I must tell you of the trouble yet to come, of the great world change."

Yasheya glowed with inner light, a storm newborn, yet his ears were not dulled. He listened.

"Strangers come into the land below. They will take the land of your people. They will point the people to a new home in the West, but no home will be there for them. But life will go on. The people will survive as they have in the past. But in the time to come, a thing grows, an evil, that no one may live through. A cloud, a brown toadstool, with sky poison, it stalks the days to come. It lives in a forest of arrow trees aimed at the moon. Someday the strangers will shoot these thick arrow trees at the moon, for these men are maddened by life. The arrow trees will catch the poison of falling stars and come back down on their houses and the houses of all the world. All will die, the human people, the animal people, the reptile and the bird people. Even mother earth's holy hair, the grass, will die and the river of life will stain with a big death and the earth, wounded, will weep."

"Who are these strangers?"

"Human beings."

"Creatures like my mother?" asked Yasheya.

"Different in skin but the same, so I think."

"If they are like my mother, as you have told me of her, they would not do this," said Yasheya.

The old one shook with sudden pain. "It is when they are not like your mother, that they allow terrible evil in the world. A mother does not poison its young."

"What is to be done?"

"You must help save the heart of the world. You must tell the people where the heart of the earth is, and knowing that, the evil will go away."

"How?" asked Yasheya, fearing what he could not understand. "I am small. The world is big. I am only one being."

"NO!" cried the old shadow man with passion. "You are all the things that walk the earth. You are strong with the hearts of many. You only need to know how to unlock the power, to summon the thunder and lightning heart of mother earth itself!"

"If you knew this power, if it dwelt in you, why could you not save the world and all the people in it?" asked Yasheya.

"Because I was not human," said the shadow man. "I am just a creature of the old flesh of mother earth and I am powerless against the destroyers. It takes a human heart and human will to stay the hand of the world slayer.

"Will you do this thing?" asked the old man. "You must join with those who fight against the evil. Wedded with their desire, you would be the hope of the world."

"Is that my place in the world? Why me? Why am I chosen for this?" asked Yasheya.

"Many are chosen, many must choose. You have power and need only to know the secret of its use."

"Teach me to summon the power and I will," said Yasheya. "For unknown world that it is to me, I am restless and must have some place in it."

The old one started to lift his arms to the sky, to ask the thunder and lightning for the great and terrible words that give birth to power.

But the thing that called the old man was stronger, and he toppled, falling back into the dust, into the cold ashes of the extinguished fire.

Yasheya took shadow father in his arms and the old one struggled to speak with his last breath. "Learn to be . . . a human being. The secret is . . ."

The old shadow man's voice faded into nothingness.

The wind died in the night and a shadow disappeared on a moonless sky.

"Come back, shadow father!" cried Yasheya, imploring the dark night. "Don't leave me! Be a human being? Is that the secret? SHADOW FATHER! HOW AM I TO KNOW?"

Yasheya's question echoed down the mountain, but the cold ashes of the fire were all that marked the passing of the old one.

Yasheya was alone.

CHAPTER SIX

With a strangely aching heart, Yasheya walked down the side of the mountain. An ancient rat enemy rode on his shoulder, invisible, all-seeing, hoping to cause the final pain.

Another pain, rode in Yasheya's heart.

He was on a journey with cold friends.

He saw the world with a thousand animal eyes and heard a thousand animal voices in the wind, but none of them saw how or spoke how he could become a human being.

He walked down into the world of his forgotten past.

He had within him a great answer but no question to unlock it.

He passed the borders of the wild places and entered the world of men.

He learned their ways and as much of their languages he did not yet know. He tried to be one of them, to be as they were.

For he sought a secret. In the new tongue, he asked all he met, how to be a human being.

They did not understand him and he got no answer. And struggled all the more blindly among them.

If he did not learn the answer to that question, he learned many other things. They were things written in the sad face of a mother losing her firstborn, things written in a boy's first observed bravery or cowardice. He learned lessons of despair and hope and shame and sorrow. In the people he met, he found kindness and cruelty in equal measure. He found wisdom and stupidity, greed and selflessness.

The shield of his own life was formed on a frame and that frame was the will of a man, wanting to be human and not knowing how.

As he built the shield of his life from the lives of those around him, the sun and rain of their lives stretched the frame, changing its shape beyond Yasheya's willed guiding.

Though Yasheya began upon a firm frame, the hide of his experience tautened and twisted until he was not as he willed himself to be.

He was a wild animal skin, tormented into the only shape it could be, human, as the pattern was once and for all time woven.

Long was his struggle to be human.

When a great storm lashed the village of his people, Yasheya walked the night, looking for answers in the wind and storm. Rain and wind tore at the roofs of the lodges, like stinging whips. Lightning crashed to earth in great anger. Thunder cracked the stone faces of the great mountains.

He was among his people but not truly of them, so he believed. In the face of the storm, he sought the face of another, the shadow being that was his father.

"Father in the sky, why do you hate me?" he cried into the teeth of the stinging wind. "Why have you abandoned me?"

The storm was the only answer he got. And he wept in the cold and he felt not half so cold on the outside as he felt inside.

He tried to stare into the heart of the lightning, to see the secret face of the thunder. He tried to embrace that cold lover, the powers of sky and night.

"Shadow father," he called out and his heart was breaking. "I have seen into the hearts of human beings. I journey now with them into the great dark. Shadow father, why did you not tell me how terrible the world is?"

Did a shadow answer him?

Yasheya thought he heard a voice in the thunder.

Yes, a voice. Asking a question in shadow father's voice.

"What is so terrible about the world?" asked the thunder.

"Becoming a human being!" cried Yasheya, seeking answers.

But the thunder never spoke to him again of becoming a human being, because he had become one.

CHAPTER SEVEN

"This game does not please me," said the ancient rat. "Only blood pleases me. Must I see all of your life? I grow hungry."

The old man laughed in the dark and his shadow turned around three times in the corner, looking for a comfortable place for a wolf to sleep.

The rat jumped back, his eyes glaring red with hate, his tail like a dark snake dragging in blood.

"Come play with my teeth, friend rat," said the wolf, and slowly began moving toward the dark scurrying one.

"See my true face," growled the wolf. "Feel the crushing strength of my jaws."

And leaping, the wolf Yasheya, seized his ancient enemy in his gaping jaws and shook the hated one. But the rat was like sand in his teeth and slipped from his grasp.

But the rat, taken by surprise, had not escaped uninjured.

Before the shape-changing escape, the wolf had heard the dry-twig snap of bones.

The rat limped to a corner of the room, eyes glaring balefully in the hideous dark. Its thick yellow tongue licked its shoulder, already stiffening with the broken bones in it.

"You've hurt me," said the rat of death. "Wolf child, through all the centuries, though many have tried, none have fought me as you have done, and done as you have done."

"I have just begun," snarled the wolf Yasheya. "I mean to snap your rotten backbone. I'll tear your head off, friend rat, go into final darkness with the foul taste of your rotted flesh on my tongue."

The wolf began to move again, clever as the stalking moon and lightning-swift in the dark.

But rat was far from dead.

"Her name. What was her name?" asked the dweller in night.

Yasheya opened his wolf jaws, poised to spring, to strike with killing force.

The ancient eater of the dead made no move to escape.

"She of the newborn dead. Tell me her name, Yasheya. Does not her life call to your life? Even now!"

The wolf hesitated and the rat moved in the dark, circling to the left.

"Remember her as she was, Yasheya," said the rat.

The wolf stood still in the center of the ruined room of the pueblo.

"Where are your sharp teeth now, Yasheya?" asked the rat with triumph. "I await your coming but you do not seem to be here any longer. Where are you, wolf? Do you journey back to see her?"

The wolf lowered his head. Yasheya, bleeding in the dark, cried out, "NO! NOT THAT!"

"I see her now, in your eyes and in your heart." And the rat moved forward, limping in triumph.

The wolf seemed to grow feeble in the dark. His back legs wobbled and then he fell to the floor. His breathing was shallow and hoarse.

He whined once as if in great pain and then slowly rolled over on his side. The wolf Yasheya could no longer hold up his head.

"Wait for me, Yasheya. I'll bring someone to meet you, someone who waits for you."

The rat turned and scurried away, limping back down the dark tunnel from where it had first come, back to its dark, foul nest of death.

Yasheya tried to put out a hand to touch the dying body of the wolf that was himself but he was too weak.

The wolf stopped moving, his legs stiffening in death. He sighed his last and final breath. He began to dissolve in the pool of Yasheya's blood.

"Magic, do not forsake me," cried Yasheya. "Thunder and lightning, hear me, and dance yet in me!"

Outside the pueblo, the sky darkened. Black clouds began to climb the heavens. First the thunder crashed and Yasheya felt a new storm in his bones, surging with new life.

Lightning struck the ruined roof of the pueblo and set it afire. It struck again and again and each place it struck, new fires sprang up.

"I thank you for not forsaking me! Burn, storm-brought fire, eat me and enemy rat," said Yasheya. "And dying, I shall yet, in fire, win over my ancient enemy!"

In the tunnel, the rat moved eagerly, despite the stiffening shoulder. Its great hunger was about to be appeased, and hunger made its journey quick.

It pushed something white and round ahead of it, something topped with black strings.

Rat poked its head into the ruined room, seeking its prey.

Above, the fires raged, beginning to eat downward into the walls.

Yasheya smiled in secret triumph.

"I've brought someone for you. A final comfort for you in your last defeated hours," said the ancient one, and the vile creature shoved the object out of the tunnel into the room.

It hit the floor with a soft thud and rolled toward Yasheya.

It was a snow-white skull with traces of black hair.

A turquoise-studded hair tie still bound up the sides of the dead hair. The blue-stone ornament gleamed in the dark, as undimmed and unchanged in its beauty as it was on the long-ago day when Yasheya had placed it gently in her hair.

His hands had shaken when he tied it on for the last time before the earth closed over her forever.

And Yasheya's wolf mouth spoke her human name once again, and it was the death of sleep and a forgetting.

And she lived in him again.

CHAPTER EIGHT

She was like she was in the first summer, almost a child, but still a woman.

Yasheya put his arms around her in the dark and she was like she had always been. It was the greatest wonder of all. With one touch, all of the glory of having been with her returned.

His hand played in the net of her thick black hair, embroidering stars into it from the nights of their lives together.

"Are you sorry we never had little ones?" she asked as they lay in the soft summer grasses and held each other tenderly.

"No," said Yasheya. "If I were human, we might have had children, but I am not, so the fault is mine and mine alone. But it is something I do not mind, for I had you, and you were enough. All any man would want."

"You seem human enough to me," she said, and she kissed him softly on the cheek.

"If I were a human being I would know how to use the power I have been given. I use it, as it uses me, but I am not human, as my shadow father was not, so I cannot do the one great thing my power was shaped to do. I have failed in this as my shadow father has failed in his teaching of me," said Yasheya, and he felt desire and longing for her rising in his youth-quickened blood.

"I wish we had all the nights of the world, to be just here, together like this," she said.

"The world may end someday because I could not be human. My shadow father was a storm. I was to be both human and world-saving storm but I am neither," said Yasheya with sorrow.

"Yasheya, you must stop punishing yourself. You are as human as I," she said, and her tears were hot on his face as she pressed against him.

Her long black hair seemed to caress him as her head rested on his shoulder. His heart was burning with a stealing tide of great feeling.

"Yasheya, if you are not a human being, then you can never die."

"Perhaps," he said, looking up into the night. "Maybe it is my path. To wander forever, to never know the rat bite of death, to be neither human nor storm, and being neither, roaming forever between the two worlds."

She rose up next to him, coming up level with him. She forced him to stare into her eyes.

He held her tightly and he saw that her eyes were burning with tears, soft as the sugar moon. Yasheya's own eyes filled strangely with tears that had never fallen in his life.

"Search your heart, Yasheya. If you are not human, now in my eyes you will find that you are not. If you are human, tell me with the truth that can only be spoken in the language of the wolves, tell me if you love me."

Yasheya stared deep into her eyes, losing himself as completely now as he had lost himself that first day so long ago when she had given birth to her dead child and he had held her for the first time.

"If you are a human being, tell me that you love me. But speak to me in the language of the wolves, which never lies," she said. "I will not know the words, but my woman's heart would know the true meaning."

"And if I cannot tell you that?" said Yasheya, afraid of what he might say in a language that held no lies.

"Then I will leave you," she said, and the hot tears rolled down her face and melted his heart.

In the tongue of his mother wolf of time past, Yasheya said, "I love you."

The words were true.

But the white skull Yasheya clutched in a gruesome embrace could not hear his words.

Only friend rat had ears in this darkness.

"You know you are a human being now and so must die. I could not beat you until you knew what you are, remembered what you had become," said the rat, and his teeth found Yasheya's flesh.

The rat of death was ready to begin.

"My magic! My power! All gone!" cried Yasheya, dying in the merciless dark.

And he wept blood.

After the thunder, after the lightning, came the gentle rain.

It fell like the tears of a woman, caressing the earth, putting out the fires in the roof of the ruined pueblo.

Yasheya's last magic was gone.

"I lost all my power because of a woman," said Yasheya, feeling his bones crumbling in the dusty mouth of the ancient rat. But even in that moment of despair, he remembered many things then, things of a life lived, and a great light seemed to shine in the growing dark.

The rat opened its mouth, its wicked teeth gleaming. It spoke. "You lost only a lie and gained a truth in its place. Your unanswered secret, was only to know how to be human, and only a woman could see it for you. Now, perhaps, it is too late, for you must die, and who else in the world will learn it?"

The rat was starving, ravenous, crawling up Yasheya's body to the soft flesh of the neck.

Yasheya tried to raise himself, to meet death standing on his feet.

The ancient rat enemy, squealed in alarm, falling back in fear, as if some unsuspected magic was about to overtake him.

But the magic was gone.

Yasheya got halfway up and could go no farther.

He raised up one arm, looking up at the face of shadow father, trying to take hold of the old one's shadow hand in the dark.

His legs gave way and as he fell, he whispered to shadow father.

"Did I have such great glory in life?" asked Yasheya, riding the cold fist of the north wind into the last storm.

The ancient one feasted.

"Yes. Yes," said shadow father, now riding on the back of the ancient rat.

"You were a human being."

The Voice of a New Instrument

Two shamans were eating together in their lodge. Katua was blind and Quetzal could only see things that were not there.

"I do not know what you call light," said Katua, "since I only see darkness."

"I call light the first inviter. It is just a spirit that shakes its hand against us, and scorning us, says our lives as shamans never tasted true passion, only pretense," said Quetzal.

A strange sound came to them. Katua opened the door to the lodge so that he might see better with his blind eyes, what had made the sound. It seemed to be a bird calling to its mate but it was a sound unlike any bird call they had ever heard before.

"An omen stalks us," said Quetzal. "I can tell you what it means if you can describe it to me."

"Yes, I see it. The blind see all too well. It is a bird of marvelous strength. It has no eyes, no feathers, no bones. It is made only out of sound, clear and high and echoing on the wind."

"If that is what kind of bird it is," said Quetzal, "then it foretells the death of us both."

"A pity," said Katua. "I am not ready to die now, having yet to acquire the desire to be ready to live."

"It is always death when one hears the voice of a new instrument," said Quetzal. "All things new require the death of old things. We are old things in this world."

"I am barely born," protested Katua. "I am so new to the world that I don't even have all my flight feathers."

"Yes, you are so young you are still an egg." Quetzal laughed. "You always tried to leave the nest wearing it. That is why you have failed in life."

"If I have failed in life, I will succeed in death," said Katua. "But you are no better than me. You too have failed."

"Perhaps before we die, we might redeem ourselves. We

might yet cover ourselves in glory. Let us rush outside and try to catch the voice of a new instrument, that bird with no body that never flies."

They rose up on their skeletons and ran for the door of the lodge. As they ran, they hit a painted gourd filled with water and it tipped over and fell. The water in the gourd moved with a special rhythm, threatening to become rain.

They ran insensibly, the sudden fever of their desire to see driving their legs down the path toward the sound of the bird that was not there.

As the bird sang, Katua fell into a fever dream, from which there was no waking.

In the dream he saw the coming of the white man.

Katua met an ocean of drowned pale children crawling blasphemously across the floor of once green land. There was a red snake there in the dream and one pale child was trying to pull out its eyes to have something pretty to play with.

In the pale child's hand, a shiny crucifix gleamed and gave off a strange light that did not belong in Katua's world. And the animals in the forest burst into flame.

And white-skinned child used the crucifix like a digging stick, and Katua dreamed through each slow century of its coming, and through each year of the dream, spectral burial racks rose up like an obscene many-treed forest, each burial tree, bearing rotting, pink, once human fruit.

In the dream, that sang in Katua's blood, was the vanishing of his own people, the long slow cold-as-a-snake's-belly death of a hundred hundred stolen years.

He saw the spread of the white man from one end of the continent to the next. He saw the burial grounds of his people turned into parking lots. Where once he read the future in the warm entrails of a dying animal whose life touched his life, he saw now in their place, new metallic engines, shiny machineries of night, placed by cold hands in the changed bodies of animals, or wired into the heads of a new race of men.

He saw his young wife of long ago, hitched to a plow, turning over the rich dark ground of mother earth, exposing to view authentic, hand-crafted souvenirs, the last ones available before the desert.

His eyeless heart filled with the last tidal wave of a shaman's life. Katua, once devoted to an unrelenting search for a warrior's honor and glory, for what would never be, stared into a darkness, as deep as death and more terrifying than blindness.

And the dream made his heart walk upon the ground.

When the bird stopped singing, Katua found himself alone, the last of his kind.

He saw a vision and in that prophecy he was building his own burial rack.

"This is strange. This that has passed before me does not release me to honor. My own survival in the face of all deathness, becomes an unforgiving cowardice. In truth, it steals my bones, while I still stand in them," said Katua. "I am dead, the last to die, so now I have to bury myself."

He shook his head, disapproving. "This is not how I wanted life to go for our people. I am too insignificant to be our stopping place. Still, if I am the last, I must leave some kind of monument for a vanished people."

He took a sharpened stick, fire-hardened, and plunged it into his body until it touched bone. On the bone, he etched an epitaph.

HERE LIES THE LAST INDIAN
HE WAS THE LAST OF HIS KIND
HE DIED OF ONESOMENESS

Katua went back into the lodge to find a suitable pair of pants to wear to bury himself in. He managed to catch the painted gourd of water that he and Quetzal had knocked over in their haste to leave the lodge. He caught it before any water was spilled.

He arrived back in the lodge before he had left.

It was not death or birth, he experienced, but a place on another part of the circle of life.

He buried himself in the womb of his mother, nicely arrayed in his best burial pants.

Later, like a lizard casting off his tail, he was born shaped in a new fire, kissed into life as a healthy baby girl, who would someday grow to be a woman who could sing like birds no one could see.

Quetzal chased the bird with such skill and speed that he passed it on the path.

The voice of a new instrument, having fallen behind him, seemed to spare his life.

He did not die in the Indian world, he lived on in the white world.

That was a kind of death too.

As he passed the bird on the path, a flash of dawn lightning struck him and he stumbled on the winding path and almost fell.

He experienced the kind of birth ecstasy that comes but seldom to a man. He was dead in one world and born again in the window of another one. It was a window that looked out, but never looked back.

He found himself surrounded on all sides by people who could not see him. He cried out to them, as if asking, What strange place am I in? But they could not hear him.

He looked around for Katua, but of him, there was no sign and almost no memory.

"Sadness seems to chase me," said Quetzal to the people who would not listen. "I face nothing, come from nothing."

Quetzal walked through fire and ice until he passed entirely through the window, jumped forever into a strange land. Once there, he danced to other voiced, unancestral music, beyond the warm kind world of green he once knew.

A white man, who saw him less clearly even than the people who could not see him at all, got him a job working high steel.

His new feathers were riveted on his back.

Quetzal walked no more in the land he had once come from.

Katua, when old, having reared many children, sat in grandmotherly splendor in the wisest councils of the people.

She had great dreams, and powerful visions. But not every dream is truth, and not all visions are prophecy. She talked of Quetzal, the one turned white who had disappeared and who would someday return.

Quetzal had great metal feathers on his back and one day, so her visions proclaimed, he would walk among the people again and raise them to greatness.

Unaware of the dream, and powerless to bring it, Quetzal raised seventeen-story monuments to someone else's dream.

Katua died alone and was buried in the ground far from her many children and the dream of Quetzal's return which had betrayed her.

Quetzal became the voice of a new instrument.

And walked uncaring over Katua's grave, singing a conquistador song.

And now, to the sounds of a new instrument, we all become birds that no one can see.

So That Men Might Not See

The jaguar woman sang a night song. It dripped out of the dark-boned flute like black blood, reeking of beauty that the sun never sees. All around her, the men of the village danced and played and sang, sometimes to a tune she called, and sometimes when their spirits were strong, they danced to music only they could hear. But not often, for her power, born of great beauty, was great and seemed to smother them. Like the prey of some great spider, they dangled from her silken web.

At night, she took her dances inside the scalp house, into a hidden room, bleak and ancestral, so that the men could not see. So that men could not see her strength was only beauty.

The dark bone flute was forbidden. Only the woman could play it.

When the ceremony of the dark flute was played in the day, the men had to lock themselves in their lodges, eyes closed against a magic they could not see. The sound of it, was like a waterfall of blood, like the cry of a bird tearing at the dead flesh of its prey.

Only the women were allowed outside then, women dressed in forbidden jade, in cloaks made of woven sky and brilliantly hued feathers from birds no man had ever seen. Here, in private splendor, the women danced and traced patterns in the warm earth, that all men are blind to.

If a man by accident or design, saw the dark flute, the flute carved from the bones of old lovers, the women seized him and dragged him into darkness. There they raped him and put his eyes out. And left him to burn in the unseen sun, the seeds of sight and male vision, killed in him. Such were the ways of the women.

The beast in the ground, the great dark crawling, yearning thing, that stirred in the dust of a thousand thousand years, knew nothing of this, only the faint sound of the song, that dark, throbbing heartbeat of women singing.

But the beast stirred in its grave, not alive, not dead, just there, pulsing with a sense of its own strangeness. It came out of the ground, rose up and came slithering down on the village, drawn by the sound of women singing.

It came close to the village but stayed a way off, watching. The great beast saw what men must not see.

The grace of the women dancing, displeased the dark one, for its own movements were the slow, dragging shuffle of the half-dead. The clear sweet sound of their flutes, made the beast angry, for its own voice was only the dry rasp of death, rattling in a monstrous throat.

Enraged, the beast crept down on the women, scheming their destruction.

He clothed himself in the flesh of a man. He sent forth a great wind and asked of the spirits how he might end the noise and grace of womankind.

A shadow spirit sat on his shoulder, the father of lies who only knows truth. "What would you ask of me, ugly beast?"

And the loathsome creature asked, "I would spoil the grace of women. I would make an end to the tyranny of their beauty. I would drown out the sweet sound of their singing."

"You must drown the wave in a bigger wave. Deep inside, in the writhing center, in the blackness, is such a sound, such a wave that can drown out the sound and beauty of women."

The dark beast turned inward, fell through the black abyss until in the depths of his own vitals, he saw what he sought, felt the great dark sting that uncoiled itself.

The beast tore the sting from the center of its backbone, tore it out of the reeking flesh.

"I shall make a thing for men. A great bull-roarer! A noise that will drown out the sound of women."

Having said that, he left to make a bull-roarer. It took a night and a day and a night. When it was ready, the great beast went into the village and attacked the women with it.

Adorned in feathers and forbidden jade, he fell upon the flute-playing women. As he got close, he whirled the great bull-roarer around his head.

The sound of it broke the graceful dancers, set them on fire and women and children ran screaming before the onslaught. Beauty fading, the bodies of women and children were singed by the great male sound.

The sting terrified them, set the women and children ablaze, burned them, blackened them, until blistered and torn and songless, they lay within the skin of their houses, near death and driven to hide.

"Yes, hide in your aging houses!" cried the great beast. "For this is the new killing sound of men, and the sight of you offends me!"

The sound of the bull-roarer was a wave that washed over the world and touched the sun, so mighty was it. The flutes of the women lay shattered in the dust.

Slowly, joyously, the men came out of their houses, and began dancing on the broken bones of the once beautiful flutes, grinding them into dust.

The sky filled with the sting of death. And the men began to dance the first war dance.

Inside the houses, robbed of grace and beauty, silenced, women sat in a new shadow and cried for children not yet born. Cried because the sound of the bull-roarer was the sound of something new and dark and terrible in the world that grace and beauty had no power against.

It was the sound of war.

Men in their stupidity, had brought it.

Women in their beauty, could not stop it.

White Fox Talks About the End of the World

When I was born, the clouds danced above me like angry deer in a forest of silver and the sun sand-painted the sky with sacred earth colors.

Then it rained like hell for two days.

I tried to tell this to my grandfather, White Fox. It happened on the day I meant to leave Cheyenne and go to New York to find my father, Elk Too Tall to Go Through the Sky, who had been missing for twenty years or more.

"I remember when the clouds danced like angry deer in a silver something or other and the sun sand-painted the sky with I forget what. And then it rained like hell for two days."

The old man wasn't having any of it.

"When you talk, a horse lifts up its tail," said the old man. "You are too young to remember your birth. Also you are too young to remember your dreams," said White Fox. "Just as I am now too old to have any new ones."

My grandfather, White Fox, is very wise for someone who isn't even here.

He just sat there cross-legged, like the picture of him they had once used on a box of cigars, and stared at nothing, looking out the shack's only window at the empty land of the reservation. He could see miles and miles of nothing. When you get to our reservation, it's the only thing that is not scarce. There is sure a lot of nothing to go around.

"Today is the time of going away," he said. "Always for us Indians, is the time of going away."

"Are you talking about me going away, you dying, or the end of the world?" I asked, counting the choices on my fingers.

"Both," said White Fox.

"Which both?"

"Both both," said White Fox, whose math was not much better than his English.

"You are a crazy old man," I said because it was true. "And you are probably right. Also nothing can be done about it. So why worry?"

"What do I worry about? I worry about nothing, because like every Indian ever born, I am not even here."

White Fox was a disappeared person, or so he claimed. Grandmother always agreed he was right about that, so I always believed it too. By a disappeared person, I do not mean he was a person who had simply picked up and left. I mean, he was a person who had ceased to exist.

I don't know if White Fox ceased to exist forever, like most of the Indian tribes that once lived in North America, or if he ceased to exist in a temporary way like a white man's promise made in a treaty.

White Fox can be a confusing person to deal with. I have always been puzzled by his disappearance. Grandmother would never explain it either, no matter how often I asked.

I suppose I could have asked Grandfather about it, but his disappearance made it impossible.

"I think tomorrow, or maybe even today, I am going to travel to New York and find my father, Elk Too Tall to Go Through the Sky," I said, and I offered the old man a cigarette.

"Why look for trouble? Why chase problems?" said the old man. "Being lost is the best thing your father ever did. It is the only thing he ever did right. Twenty years is one very good lost. Why want to spoil his aim? Maybe he is not wanting to be found and ruin his one good thing?"

The old man took the cigarette and put it between his yellow teeth and munched it the way a horse nibbles grass.

The old man ate two packs of cigarettes a day. He especially liked the kind with filters. He said the crunchy part always made him lick his lips.

Well, maybe White Fox was right about my father. A man gets lost, sometimes it's because he wants to. My grandfather is often right, which is not surprising for someone who has ceased to exist. When you are no longer around, you can afford to be right.

"I think maybe later I am going to lay down on my stomach and die dead," said the old man, putting his hand out for another cigarette. The shreds of the last cigarette were still clinging to his teeth. "Maybe in an hour, maybe less."

"Even if it's messing up my father's only thing done good, I am still going to New York. There's things I want to ask him about. Personal things."

"Did I say you shouldn't? Besides, better you go. You always did annoy me most of all. You always asked the worst questions of anyone I ever knew. You would probably ask me a dumb question when I am lying on my stomach, dying myself dead."

"I am sorry to see you die so early in the day. If you could have held off till this afternoon, David Round Fox was maybe going to come over with some beer," I said, telling him the latest rumor.

The old man looked disgusted.

"That no-good Round Fox. That is just like him to go buy beer and then not show up till too late for me to drink it. When I think of all the cigarettes he smoked of mine all these years, must have been hundreds I could have eat myself, why, I can hardly stand not to want to knock him down with my fists."

Grandfather looked all around the house. There wasn't much to see. Maybe eight thousand empty cigarette packs in one corner and a bunch of old Indian souvenirs, which we had made in Hong Kong so we could sell them to white tourists at six times their original cost.

There was no furniture in the house because the old man had always insisted that a house should be open enough to ride a horse through.

Every once in a while White Fox would ride a horse through it, just to see if it was the kind of house he wanted to live in.

Grandmother had a house of her own because Grandfather didn't exist, and she wasn't about to have a stupid old man who didn't exist riding his horse through her house.

Me, I always thought she was probably right to do that. It is difficult to live in a house that is full of running horses.

Even one running horse makes it difficult.

Now that Grandfather was ready to die, there was a lot of stuff suddenly to take care of.

I looked out the window at the sun to see what time it was.

That is how Indians tell time. It is one of the special talents passed on to me by my people. From the position of the sun overhead, I knew that it was Tuesday.

White people do not have this gift. All they can ever tell about the time from looking at the sun, is that, if they can see it, it must not be night.

But I, full of my own Indianness, and impatient to get to New York, knew it was Tuesday. Well, maybe Tuesday or Wednesday. Sometimes Tuesday looks a lot like Wednesday.

It was already getting pretty late in the day, whether it was Tuesday or Wednesday, so I thought I better find out how quick I could wrap this death thing up.

"This dying thing. Are you going to go quick or are you going to linger?"

The old man shrugged. "It don't matter to me. I could go like that." He tried to snap his finger, but it was so old and brittle, it broke.

"Yeeow!" cried White Fox, waving his broken finger in the air. "That hurt like a porcupine in the face!" He held the crooked finger up in front of his eyes. "That is what is so nut-crazy about getting old. Is no goddamn junkyard where you can get spare parts."

White Fox put his finger on the floor, took one boot and deftly smashed the finger under his foot. The finger straightened out, but not without hurting even more. The old man's eyes bugged out and his false teeth fell into his lap.

White Fox took his foot off his finger. It was straight now, but beginning to swell up. He stuck his teeth back in his mouth and flexed his jaw until they were back in place.

I was going to ask White Fox why go to all the bother since he was going to lie down and die pretty soon, but he waved his sore hand at me.

"Need fingers straight for last big magics. Got to leave recorded message for next generation. Big curse and prediction of future and other kinds of noise," he said by way of explanation.

Now I was in for it. Grandfather was going to do every last damn piece of business there was. It was going to take one long forever.

"Couldn't we maybe skip most of that and get to the good stuff right away?"

The old man sneered. "Tough news! We go through all the business, so shut up already."

I sighed.

"What do you want me to do?"

"Bring me the lower hair of a virgin," said the old man.

I rolled my eyes and stared at the sky, which was easy to see through the bullet holes in the shack roof.

Grandfather often killed flies on the ceiling with his rifle. It helped relieve the boredom. Doing this was about all the excitement there was to be had on the reservation.

It was also a sure-fire way to kill flies because White Fox was a good shot, but it was kind of hard on the roof, which was pretty well shot away by now.

"The lower hair of a . . . You have got to be kidding," I said, regarding him suspiciously. You have to be careful when dealing with people who aren't there.

The old man laughed. "I was just trying to see if you were awake. This dying is very funny and very serious business, so you try and stay awake all through the whole damn thing. That is my final wish. Try not to fall asleep until I am pretty well deaded up."

The old man suddenly belched, and a partially digested cigarette filter popped out of his mouth.

The old man frowned. "Damn! I got less time that I thought. I better do this whole thing pretty damn quick!

"Get me a tomahawk. And a war lance. Also some bald eagle feathers and . . ." The old man tucked his hands under his armpits, trying to think of what he needed. ". . . and, OK, need some bear grease. Also fire from mesquite and willow branches."

He remembered something else. "Also need two arrows and a bowl of deer blood."

"Maybe you should just keep on living," I said. "What do you think I am, supermarket of museum curiosities?"

The old man got angry. Maybe he was angry. His face was all screwed up. Maybe he just had a stomachache from too many cigarette filters.

"OK, smart-nose grandson, just do the best you can. Just don't take one long goddamn forever! I got big urge to go on my stomach."

Well, I did the best I could. I found a tomahawk and a war lance and some feathers in the tourist souvenirs. I couldn't find bear grease but I did find a bottle of sheep dip, which was close enough, I hoped.

The fire to be made from mesquite and willow branches was too much, though. Used to be stuff like that all over the place, but that was before we discovered anything chopped up fine enough could be sold to white tourists as Indian tobacco. We even lost a couple wooden outhouses that way in the height of the tourist season.

So lacking the special kind of wood and all that, I used my pocket cigarette lighter and set fire to a bunch of old moccasins made in Hong Kong, still in their boxes. They were supposed to be made of genuine deerskin but mostly they were some kind of plastic, so they burned like crazy.

Grandfather looked at what I had brought him and curled his lips in disgust.

"You are one great big arrow in the ass, you know that? You'd have to wet yourself just to be able to find your little man spear! Is this the best you could do?"

The tomahawk and the war lance both had rubber heads. Grandfather tapped the tomahawk against his face. It bounced like a ball off his forehead.

"If I did not have to have a bowel movement at this very moment, I would be one very angry old Indian!"

The eagle feathers were really chicken feathers that had been dyed yellow and blue and green.

Grandfather stared up at the ceiling. "Well, Great Spirit, I bet you are laughing all over the sky up there. Well, you know I had the urge if not the right material to work with."

Grandfather looked down, then whispered at me, "I ain't going to tell him every little thing. Especially not about the damn chicken feathers! I figure from this distance his eyes ain't so good and if he can't take a joke, I say the dog with him!"

"You ought not to joke so much with the Great Spirit," I told him. "He may decide you are not so funny a guy. Also his funny might not be your funny."

"Fat lot you know. Me and Great Spirit used to go drink together. Me and him closed the Saddle Up bar many a time. Fact is, he can't hold his booze. I personal have drunk him on his ass! But as to his funny and my funny, why you just look out and see how absolute nut-funny whole damn world is. See me get old and big important parts of me, falling off like dead fenders on Indian car, and boy, you know, Great Spirit got more jokes than Navahos got sheep."

Grandfather waved his arms and the tomahawk struck me in the face. The old man didn't seem to notice.

White Fox tried to wave the war lance but he got the rubber end tangled up in a horse bridle hanging on the wall behind him and it fell out of his hands.

I threw more moccasins into the fireplace, which I was soon to find out was a mistake in the making. The plastic was burning a lot more enthusiastic than I realized.

It was also putting a lot of black smoke into the air, which stunk like my grandfather's feet, maybe worse.

White Fox said a couple of Indian words but he soon gave that up. He hardly ever talked Indian anymore. He claimed it made him sneeze. He went back to yelling at the Great Spirit in English.

I don't know if the part about the sneezing was a lie or not. Mostly, I think maybe it was everybody he loved who spoke the old language was dead, and he hurt less somehow in English.

"Great Spirit! I am pretty damn well out of steam! I am all dead from the neck down. I am just touching up a few last things here, then on my belly and you know all the rest. Well, this grandson of my own blood, Great Spirit, he is stupid as hell!"

"Thanks a lot," I said sarcastically.

I noticed that the fire was beginning to spread from the fireplace to the rotting wood on the floor.

"Yes, Great Spirit. My grandson is as stupid as fleas on a wooden dog," said the old man, warming to his subject.

It began quickly to look like the whole place might catch on fire. I went over and began jumping up and down on the floor, trying to put it out.

"You don't have to blab it to everybody, especially the Great Spirit," I said between jumps.

"I call 'em like I see 'em, so shut up already!" snapped the old man. "Don't interrupt me 'cause I am just getting to the most important stuff."

The old man coughed once more from the smoke.

"Now where was I?" he asked. He looked at me through the thickening clouds of black smoke. "You got the bear grease?"

I stopped stamping out the fire in the floor long enough to hand him the bottle of sheep dip.

He looked at the label and swore some hot words.

He shook his head in utter dismay, which made his nose bleed.

He noticed the blood and frowned. "Hoo boy! I am in some damn lousy shape. I better hurry damn quick! I am going so damn fast I can hardly hold my nose open!"

He poured the sheep dip on his fingers and held them up to the sky.

"You see this stuff here that is supposed to be bear grease, Great Spirit? I hope that you will pretend that it is bear grease, Great Spirit, on account I want you should grease the chute before I go sliding up it! I have lived one dog lifetime!

"I am out of ammunition. I am out of medicine. And parts are falling off. I am tired as hell." He looked down at his lap, surprise on his face. "I am also at the last minute feeling very sexy, which is, you gotta admit, a very funny funny, so before I slide up the tunnel into the sky, Great Spirit, slick it up good, OK? I don't want no splinters in my ass is why I even mention it.

"Now the funny stuff, Great Spirit, there is the matter of my grandson. I don't know why I even bother. I never saw such a stupid in my whole life!"

If I wasn't so busy trying to put out the fire I might have said something pretty sarcastic at this point. I might even have thought about hitting him but what's the use of hitting somebody who isn't even there. I'd never be sure he felt it.

"But what can I do? Blood is thicker than water as you know if you ever sat in it. He has got his grandmother's brains and my nose. What can I do?" said White Fox, shaking his head sadly.

He waved his arm, trying to get the smoke out of his face.

"Do something for him. But if it is too much trouble on account of he is so stupid, forget the whole thing."

"Thanks for nothing," I said, dancing on the fire but not quite fast enough to stay ahead of it. The bottoms of my boots were smoking.

"Where's my arrows and bowl of deer blood?" demanded the old man.

"I don't think you are going to last long enough for me to find them. You are going pretty quick," I reminded him.

The old man sighed. He looked up at the sky through the bullet holes. "Am I embarrassed, Great Spirit? You bet your ass! I could have done a big magic right at the end there but with one thing this way and that thing that way." He spread his hands in a how-could-I-help-it gesture. "Also, I got to make a bowel movement real bad, which I didn't count on, so I guess we just got to let this thing go whipping by."

His eyes began to glaze.

"Quit playing with fire!" roared the old man. "I am doing my big exit. This is a dumb time to go fooling with matches! Help me on my stomach, hurry up quick!"

I stopped fighting the fire, which was OK 'cause I wasn't winning that one anyway, and came over to help the old man.

I got hold of him and started to roll him over. "Ain't you supposed to . . . ain't the traditional way . . . well, ain't you supposed to lay on your back and aim your eyes at the sky as you die?"

"Boils!" said the old man with a wink. His eye stuck shut. With his other eye, he watched me flip him over.

"OK, clear the damn runway, I am out of gas, you bet your ass!"

The old man closed his one working eye, and died. He did this for a little while and was doing very good at it but then he had to stop.

"It's funny as hell." An eye opened, the last one still working. I could barely hear his voice. It was the tiniest of whispers.

I bent down till my head was next to his. He whispered in my ear. It seemed like an important message.

"Is David Round Fox here with the beer?"

"No, Grandfather."

"He's a horse's ass!"

I sighed. That was Grandfather. He was ornery as hell.

"You are going to end the world," he said suddenly, and then he closed his last eye and this time he died pretty much all the way.

He had a pained expression on his face, which I think was maybe the bowel movement.

He was such a terrible old rascal it probably was justice he had so much trouble at the end.

"Now what the hell did you mean by that?" I asked, which was a waste of time since he was real dead this time.

Well, I was angry. It was just like Grandfather to try to drop a lot of bad news on me with his last breath.

I didn't want to know I was going to be the one who ended the world. Who would want to know a thing like that?

Later, of course, I would be sad about the old man. I loved him a lot. As much as anyone can love anyone who isn't even there. He raised me since I was little. He had been both father and grandfather to me.

My father had been lost successfully for twenty years and my mother was only my mother when she wasn't trying to raise the dead and scare the living with the insides of her legs in the only three bars in Cheyenne, Wyoming, that hadn't thrown her out yet.

They would throw her out eventually, since she spent too much time thinking with her legs and not enough time taking baths, but till that happened, she was as gone as anybody can be gone.

That had left me to grow up with the old man who wasn't there and if you think it isn't confusing to learn to live life from a man who isn't there, you ought to give it a shot sometime and see how it does by you.

But for the moment, I was going to postpone my grief.

Mostly so I could concentrate on surviving the fire.

By the time the old man, what with stalling and everything, got himself deaded up, the whole damn place was on fire.

I had a fast few seconds there, trying to figure out just how I was going to get out of there without joining my grandfather, when one of the walls fell down and, suddenly, it was easy.

I just ran toward the wall, jumped as far as I could and landed in the dirt behind the house.

I was smoldering a little, my shirt was going pretty good, so I got rid of it quick.

I had a couple of blisters on my shoulders and my boots were no longer made for walking, but other than that, I was just fine.

The roof fell in as I was standing there. I looked back inside the house, trying to see Grandfather's body.

It was gone.

With the roof and one wall gone, I could see inside the house clearly. There was no mistaking it.

Grandfather's body was gone.

I guess, thinking about it, it was to be expected.

Grandmother always said he didn't exist.

Now I knew she was right.

Mostly then, this is just a funny story about death but it is also about disappeared persons and the end of the world, which is not quite so funny.

If you are wondering where the end of the world comes in, it was buried not very deep in my grandfather's last words. It was in his not being, not existing, going without having come.

Perhaps I have always known the bad news about Grandfather, about the end of the world, about how he became a disappeared person.

After all, what is the end of the world?

If the young don't have the old people inside them, when the old ones die, when they disappear, then the world comes to an end.

So dies the Indian world.

I woke up the next morning and I had disappeared.

As if Bloodied on a Hunt Before Sleep

The white man fancied himself a hunter of animals and men. For the animals, he carried a gun, for men he carried a college education that designated him an anthropologist.

He sat in Wolf Walker's lodge and told tales of hunting. He was establishing rapport. It was a form of barter. He told stories calculated to establish kinship. In exchange, he expected to collect anthropological hunting trophies, perhaps unrecorded legends or creation myths or simply details of Indian life as it once was lived.

He felt as much for his prey, human or animal, as any white hunter felt.

Wolf Walker was a rich man in an Indian way. He had deep knowledge of the coming from of his people. He saw much with the eyes of a shaman and it was said he could see deeper into the night than any night stalker.

He was poor in the white way and would not have eaten so well or so fully if the white man had not been there to provide the meal.

The old man chewed on a chicken bone and seemed to follow the anthropologist's story with interest.

The white man relived the attacks and combats between himself and the animals he had killed, raising his arms and acting out the parts of both hunter and hunted.

The old man ate and listened gravely. The story was punctuated by an occasional cracking sound as Walking Wolf bit down on the bones, grinding them between his teeth.

He liked the taste of the bones almost as much as he liked the meat. He thanked the Great Spirit he still had strong teeth to break bones.

When the white man's story was finished, Walking Wolf wiped his hands on a piece of torn buckskin.

The white man had a way of making his stories exciting, but wisely, his stories seldom made him out as the hero. More often than not, the animals he hunted emerged victorious in his stories. He talked of the too-clever animals that got away.

The anthropologist knew that this would tend to make him seem more sympathetic.

"I eat your food and it is good because in the days that now come to me, I am often hungry," said Walking Wolf. "Your manner of speaking is pleasant and the telling of the tales is skillful and good-eared. They are lies. These are but lies you wish to exchange for my goodwill. I do not mind. It does not trouble me. Now I will pay you for the food."

The white man shifted uncomfortably on his hard wooden chair.

"Answer me this, white man, do you think it possible that a wolf could bite a man's arm hard enough to tear his heart out?"

"It doesn't seem likely. Knowing what I know about human bodies, the arm might come off, but no, the heart ripped out, impossible, I would say."

"Then I shall tell you a story that will show that you are wrong. I do not mind telling a story that proves a white man wrong. This story I tell you is a hunting story and you seem to like hunting stories. There is much that is strange in this story. In the darkness of my old age, the thunder of this story still makes utterance to me and so it comes forth."

The white man, as unobtrusively as possible, got a notebook and pen out and laid them on his lap.

"As you have hunted and other white men have hunted in this valley for a living, there were two brothers, men of our people, who hunted more than all of you. They hunted on the dim paths of night.

"They rose up in the morning of their manhood and hunted and loved nothing else, talked only of this and lived as such shadowless souls, living their waking lives for only this. Do you know of such great passion, white man, this great fever whose tongue is the wind's tongue? This fever that I too have known." The old man's voice shook with emotion.

The old man touched his chest with a closed fist. "Yes, the great war wind of the chase sat in my chest and I made the trails of the hunted shake with my passing. So it was once, but no more.

"And even as my heart was full of the hunter's madness, the younger of the two brothers in all forms of his faces, all terrible in the light of other days, in all the works of his killing hands, he had the greater wind at his back. No, not a wind, a great storm, and his madness was a great shield.

"When first he arose, younger brother shook off the bonds of night and took on the chains of the hunt, his steps sought the wild ones and violence was his first waking thought. Each morning began with the death of a forest creature and each day ended with the quick snap of stalking death."

"I have met men like that," said the white man, quietly.

"No. Such men are gone from the world, and gone before your time and gone in my time. I do not hunt. Listen and you shall see," said Walking Wolf, and there was almost anger in his face.

"Now these two brothers I speak of were as wild as the forgotten things in the unsearchable places of the time-stricken lands. In youth, they walked large as trees, and the blood was quick in them and swift-running. They had great night-seeing eyes. And they cried the great hunting cry which comes deep-rooted in the heart like worms bred in the black bark of the tree of all trees."

The white man wrote quickly in his notebook, his hand dancing to capture each and every word.

"It was to kill that a flower bloomed within them. No woman was embraced, when death was the woman in their arms. They worshipped blood and breathed the fragrance of its long red hair." Walking Wolf looked to the four directions, reading the winds of memory and his body shook with the passing of the wind. His face was a fire, all death and all life, and his body shook again like a nation in ruin.

The white man looked up and saw the spasm seize the old man and stayed the pen in his hand, fearful that the old man would drop dead of a heart attack. But the old man calmed himself.

"In the winter of the great cold, when the stormshaker roared in the world, the great wolves became ferocious. They came down out of their lairs and roamed around our lodges and howled until even the Great Spirit trembled. They fell upon us and no person was safe from them outside his lodge. We lost children to them, we lost women to them and warriors, for their hunger was unslakable and they had lost their fear of man and our arrow-tipped death in that terrible winter."

"Eighteen forty-six," said the white man, noting the year, unaware that he had spoken aloud, for he had his own way of counting time.

"But the two brothers did not stay inside their lodges, no, for they hunted the hunters and had great joy in even more dangerous lifetaking. Many wolves fell to their arrows and spears. And sometimes, in his blood lust, the younger brother would fall upon a wolf with only his knife, for he sought always the greater madness.

"Then it came to be known that a great wolf, which had killed our children and torn the leg from a woman, was upon us. Our anguish rose and our spirits gazed dumbly upon this great beast. They say his hot breath, foul and sweet as the grave, came into the very lodges and made the home fires weak. A great warrior sought his death and left us, and returned no more, for his blood was upon the snow and the stars spelled death.

"But the two brothers were greatly uplifted in their hearts, for this was the great hunt they sought. Where fear closed the hearts of our people, they longed to walk. They set themselves on the trail of this great wolf, and nothing else in life.

"But he, the great wolf, was a ghost dancer in the scalp house. They killed two wolves, but not the great one. And each night, they brought their kills back to the lodges and found a tale of some new death the great wolf had brought. Always it happened in a place where they had not been, for he eluded them like the windigo women who lure young men into the woods to steal their bones.

"So it went, and the stormshaker would not relent and the brothers traveled farther and farther each day from their lodges and got no closer to the wolf than an arrow gets when shot at the blood-red moon.

"So it went, and all the dark night ways and hunting chants were no good against the beast. The two brothers became one great burning heart, like a many-rooted tree that swelled with hate toward the sky. In their anger came great strength, and the people of their own blood began to fear them, as they feared the great wolf. For the people looked into their eyes and saw the thing that burned in the eyes of that which they sought.

"When they had been two days gone from their lodges, following a wolf track that seemed promising, the elder brother said, 'I shall sing my death song if my knife does not soon find the heart of this beast.'

"The younger brother had already painted his face for death. 'I will kill him with teeth and bare hands or leave my bones on the burial rack.'

"So their hearts were set for death," said the old man.

The white man stirred uncomfortably in his chair but his hand continued to move across the paper, chasing the words.

"But the great wolf was not at the end of their trail," the old man continued. "And so they came back in despair to their lodge and found that the great wolf had been there. They found their aged father, ripped and half-eaten by the great wolf. It had come into their lodge and profaned it and severed the great living root of their lives." A tear formed in the corner of Walking Wolf's eyes and he seemed to shrink in his chair, suddenly old as if his twilight had come upon him.

Again the white man stopped writing and was afraid the old man would do some injury to himself.

"Perhaps we should rest for a while," said the white man. "Your throat must be dry and my hand could use a rest, too."

The old man did not seem to hear him. Walking Wolf stared at something, at a road that went backward and the white man was not on that road.

"The two brothers buried the body of their father," he said. "They took his torn and claw-ripped heart and burned it and gave it to Sky Grandfather, for the great wolf had burned their hearts and their home on earth was now ashes and dust.

"The people of the village saw them at their task and grew frightened. The brothers were more demon than flesh now, sucklings of the great wolf that none could kill, and the people hid their faces, for the brothers were no longer good to look upon.

"And the brothers fired their lodge, for they lived now only in the hoped-for corpse of the great wolf. His ribs were now their lodge pole. They set out after him, hot now upon his trail, red with the blood of their father."

The white man wrote furiously, for now the words came faster and the old man was in some kind of fever himself and could not be stopped.

"As they chased him, day chased night and caught it, but the great wolf was in the next day. The trail was seared with the fever of their passing. The shaper of thunders would have hid from them, if he had seen their faces. On they ran, and the next day fell to the thunder of their feet and the straining of their lungs and the ache in their hearts, but the great wolf was always in the next night, or so it seemed.

"And then, at the edge of the night, when their hearts were about to burst, a great fear rattled in their chests and darkness took hold of them with icy hands.

"The younger brother said, 'Our strength is going and the beast mocks us.'

"The elder brother said, 'We hunt a demon, smarter than men. We are dead men already and he has not yet given us our death. As we would give it to him.'

"The moon came up and ahead of them, on the trail, sat the great wolf, waiting for them. And the younger brother looked at the moon and said, 'The sun is blinding me. It steals the sleep from my eyes and hides it in a spider's web.'

"His hands uncurled and became claws, making killing motions.

"And the fear of madness and the fear of the wolf were mixed in the heart of the elder brother, and his weapons were ashes and dust, and his hands would have made the sign for peace but he had never learned it. He made a fist of his hands and found the ashes of his father's burned heart in it, and so mocked, the fear ran from him and the old hunger was new born.

"The elder brother would have moved then but he saw something the younger brother could not see. The death of all deaths in the moon glow and a moon shadow crept over him and froze him like a dead tree. And he could not move.

"But younger brother saw only a mad dawn and burned in the blazing sun, soul destroyed.

"Younger brother ran toward the wolf and the wolf sat like a golden fire, all tangled and scorched with the worms of death.

"And they met and locked in great combat, the wolf ripping and clawing and the younger brother, a ravening wind mad with hunting lust, stabbing for the heart of the terrible one.

"Long did they struggle and the blood was a river.

"Out of that river flowed the life of the younger brother. The great wolf seized him by the face, the black jaws came together and the skull was crushed. Younger brother dropped to the ground under the weight of his death and the wolf moved back, ran away howling with fierce wild joy. It stopped upon the path and waited for the sun to rise in the heart of the elder brother."

The white man was covered with sweat, writing furiously, his shoulders hunched forward over the notebook. His arm ached and his fingers were a searing, fierce pain.

Walking Wolf was bent like a man facing a great wind. His eyes burned like two knife wounds and his face was contorted like a man in the grip of something dark.

"And so I," said Walking Wolf, "the elder brother, on legs that felt like betraying me, moved forward then. I took tiny steps like a child, like a deer child first walking toward newborn milk. The trees seemed to touch me with icy clawed hands and something was in me, a stain on my heart. Was it fear that ripped me? Was that knife in me now, that had never feared, that had painted my face for death?

"I stood in the blood of my dead brother, and the trail of the great wolf seemed cold and lifeless before me. The wolf awaited my coming but I did not come. I knelt beside the slain one and took his lifeless body and held it against me. Death of the hunted, that had always been my strength, but it vanished as I held my dead brother."

Tears streamed down the face of the old man and his voice cracked with an old longing, a sorrow that scaled a long-ago sky.

"I moved his hands so that the weapons fell from them, for in death he still had his feet set to climb the hunter's path. I held his torn face against me, made and broken, slain and forgiven by the great wolf's stronger way. And it was a face without peace or kindness, and it was not good to look upon, for it was my face, too."

The old man touched the wrinkled corners of his eyes, found the tears and dropped his hands, as if bloodied.

He stood there motionless on the old road and it seemed as if he would speak no more.

"What happened?" asked the white man, and there was something strange in his voice, a new emotion. His face was white and his hands had stopped moving across the page. The last of the old man's words had gone unrecorded.

"The noise of a hunter's heart!" cried the old man. "As its feathers are once spread, so it must always take flight!

"I held my death against me in my brother's body! But do young men understand death? Only for a second and never deeply enough, for revenge was in my veins and my hunter's heart still made utterance to me.

"I threw his body from me, and the trail of the great wolf burned in the sun. I stabbed my arm so the blood would know how to flow and I went toward the great wolf, singing my death song!

"He saw my great anger and knew fear, for he fled from me then. But no creature can run faster than vengeance. I ran through places men did not go and did not see them. I ran into nights unseen and days unnumbered and saw only the great wolf, living for his death or mine.

"The forest tried to hold me back, tearing at me, and my blood flowed again and again, tree and branch wounded, but I felt only the hunting wound and there is no greater pain.

"We met, that great wolf and I. In a forest of azure and ice, in a valley where the sun never shines but burns. I threw myself upon the wanderer and had the strength that comes to a man only once in his lifetime, and then comes never again. I was thunder.

"I was lightning.

"I was death in all of its faces.

"The great wolf tried to sink his claws in me, tried to rip my heart out but I threw him off. With my knife, I ripped his eyes out and we came at each other again.

"My knife was out and drove home and I meant to make a shadow of him but his jaws closed on my arm and the knife fell from my fingers. I tried to throw him off but his jaws locked and could not be forced off. My arm went around his gray neck and tightened and squeezed and then death rattled in his throat.

"The wind fell out of his empty eyes. My arm strained and I held him against me, ever tighter until it seemed I would squeeze his head off and I felt no pain from the wolf jaws fastened upon my arm.

"No pain! 'See, my younger brother!' I cried in my joy and I crushed the dead wolf against me till I thought I would pull him through my own chest.

"I had conquered him. The seed of his dark soul was dead, strangled by my hand into darkness and I looked down in triumph at his wolf face and saw my brother.

"My arm encircled his sad dead face and the wolf-bitten arm had my brother's blood on it. And the wolf was my brother dead and he was me alive. Young brother equal and one with me, man that is made of me, man that is I, Walking Wolf.

"I had been blind in the blood.

"I saw the emptiness of the hunter's life.

"In one hand one holds a passion for death. But is not wisdom another hand with a passion for life? The arrow of youth is strung on a mighty bow, but it falls in the dust.

"I felt the ache in my arm, the great wolf jaw bite, and my life-hating heart twisted in that painful flame, in that great ripping wolf bite.

"The jaws of the wolf are long and terrible and speak of love. It fastened upon my arm and tore out my heart."

Walking Wolf bowed his head, the fever had passed, leaving him old, ruined, an empty husk of a man.

"And I would hunt no more, for I had no longer a hunter's killing heart. And so, I buried my dead, but they have followed me all my days. They follow me now and I have no heart big enough to give them rest, so deeply did the wolf bite me."

The white man stared at the pages, the writing forgotten, thinking of his own life perhaps, of a hunt he had begun, of many hunts and a stalking season within himself.

The notebook had a number on it, like a notch a hunter makes to number his kills.

Walking Wolf stared at the white man, as if seeing him for the first time. The old man was full of sorrow, of remembered grief.

"That is how a wolf can bite an arm and rip out a heart," he said, and he stared down at the white man's notebook, as a hunter stares at the weapons of another to appraise their worth.

"Why is it that your hand is still?" asked the old man, "and you no longer take down in writing what you have sought?"

The white man stood up suddenly. There was a strange look on his face, a look that the old man almost understood. The white man folded the notebook up, stared at it for a moment as if seeing something else in his hand, then tossed it on the fire. It caught fire easily and began to burn.

"I stopped writing," said the white man, "because a wolf bit my arm."

The old man did not understand. "You think I lied," he said bitterly, and he pulled back the sleeve of his shirt and showed the white man the old scar the wolf had made in a time long gone.

The white man held out his arm, and rolled back his sleeve, "My scars don't show," he said. "But my heart was ripped out too."

Then the old man understood, as one hunter understands another.

He looked at the white man.

And saw the scars.

When Old Man Coyote Sang the World into Being

Of the old times, before there was any world, there lived only Old Man Coyote. There was no earth, no trees or mountains. All that there was, was water, just water everywhere.

"What shall I do?" asked Old Man Coyote. But, of course, there was no one to answer him.

So Old Man Coyote began singing to the sky and the water that was everywhere.

"I would like to know what to do," he sang.

Then he met Old Woman Coyote. She had been hiding somewhere, no one knows just where even to this day. She never gave away any of her secrets.

"What are you doing?" asked Old Woman Coyote.

"I don't know. Do you have any ideas?" asked Old Man Coyote.

"Why don't we make the world?" suggested the woman.

And so they did.

They made a song together and when they had it the way it was supposed to be, they threw it up in the sky and it became the earth.

When they looked up in the sky, they saw the earth and they said, "Let's go there right away."

And so they did, in one big jump.

They began stretching the earth with their paws. That's how they made the world. They pushed with their paws and they sang little songs as they worked. These little songs would fall to the ground and that's how we got mountains and trees, and deer people, and the fish people and all the animal peoples, all things that live in creation.

That was how everything started. That, too, was the time when Old Man Coyote put us Indians on the face of this world.

All the men and women were put upon the world.

Old Man Coyote and his wife were very pleased with what they had done.

They had made the sun shine bright in the sky. They had made the birds sing because the world was so beautiful. And it was very beautiful.

And it was that way for many, many long years.

Old Man Coyote and his wife were very happy with the world they had made. Because they were so happy, the sun always shone, the birds always sang; it was the time of forever summer.

And so it was, unchanged and unchanging.

Old Man Coyote had given a song to all the beings of creation so that they might give birth to their own kind and live forever.

It was a very good world then, for there was no death and no night and every creature of creation was at peace with all others.

But then one day there was trouble.

Every creature in the world was giving birth to its own kind. The bear had children and the bear's children had children and then they too had children. The deer had children and the deer's children had children, and so on.

Men and women had children and they had children who grew up and had children, too. Trees made seeds that grew to be other trees. Everything was growing, growing and bringing forth creatures of its own kind.

But there was no death. No death. The earth was small. Soon it was all filled up. There was no room for the new deer children, for the new bear children and for the new people children.

Even the fish children had filled up the sea so full that it was as solid with fish as ice upon a river.

What did all the peoples of creation say about this?

Old Man Coyote and Old Woman Coyote they were up in the sky just taking a nap and so they did not know about this trouble on earth.

The peoples of creation were troubled. They were beginning to find things wrong with the way it was. "Every day is the same," they said. "The sun always shines, the birds always sing, it is always summer."

Now they didn't know what was to be done. They didn't know.

So they said, "Let us call on Old Man Coyote and Old Woman Coyote, who made us. They will know what to do."

And so they made a song, and they sent it across the sky when they sang it. Well, as you can imagine, with all those thousands and thousands of peoples singing this one song, it was a very LOUD song.

It woke up Old Man Coyote and Old Woman Coyote pretty quick.

They didn't like that at all. They came jumping down to earth right away and they were pretty grouchy.

"What's wrong down here?" they both said, in that grumpy kind of voice people get when they are awakened too quickly.

But, of course, they really didn't need to ask what was wrong. The minute they landed on earth they both knew what was wrong. Why, there was hardly any room for Old Man Coyote and Old Woman Coyote to land!

"It's the same every day," said all the people. "The sun always shines, the birds always sing, it's summer forever and there are so many peoples of every kind that there is no room for new children. We want you to change it. We want you to do something about this."

Old Man Coyote looked at his wife. "What shall we do?" he asked her. Old Man Coyote was the strong one. But Old Woman Coyote was the smart one. That made all the difference.

Old Woman Coyote said, "We will have to stop the sun from shining. We will have to make the birds go away and not sing all the time. Summer will have to go. All these peoples, we can't have all these peoples. It will have to be changed."

"But how will we do that?" asked Old Man Coyote.

"I know what to do," said Old Woman Coyote. "It is one of my secrets. I will use one of my secrets and change things."

Old Man Coyote asked the peoples if that was what they wanted. "It cannot be changed once it is done," he warned them.

"Change it," cried all the peoples, "and hurry. We have been living all these years and years and we are tired of this. We need some rest."

"Very well," said Old Woman Coyote, and she drew her cloak around her so that no one could see how she used her secret.

Suddenly, the sun went dark. All the peoples were frightened, very frightened, as they did not know what this was.

It was night. That is what the darkness was.

All the peoples lay down and discovered how to sleep.

That was how the day that had lasted almost forever ended.

That was not all there was of the secret. No, it was only a little bit of Old Woman Coyote's secret.

The next morning when the sun came up, some of the peoples could not wake up.

They could not wake up.

"What is wrong?" all the peoples who had come awake cried. "Why can't these other creatures of creation get up?"

They were dead.

That was part of Old Woman Coyote's secret. Not all of it, but part of it.

The last part of Old Woman Coyote's secret came a little while later.

One morning, when the peoples woke up, all the trees had turned many colors and the leaves of the trees had fallen to the ground.

Old Woman Coyote had given them night and death and seasons.

And night and death and seasons had given everything in creation a rest.

In the winter, the birds flew away so that the people would not have to listen to them sing all the time. That was the way it was.

The birds became the special messengers of the seasons. When the birds stopped singing and began to fly away, it reminded all the peoples of creation that a season had ended. It reminded them that each person's life has a season and that one day, like summer, it must end.

And that is the way of the world Old Man Coyote sang into being.

And that is the end of the story.

Knowing Who's Dead

They were climbing a hill on the way to oblivion.

Other Indians had been there before them. More would probably follow them. Sometimes the world is built that way.

It was a small tribe consisting of two young men and one old one.

Tato and Elk Boy were carrying Natchez, the old man. They had him cradled in their arms between them.

They were making halting progress directly toward the middle of nowhere.

It is possible they have been carrying the old man ever since the world began.

Tato struggled with the weight of the old man and almost stumbled on the uneven ground.

"How far is it anyway, to the burying ground, Elk Boy?"

"I don't know, Tato. But dead people sure are heavy," said Elk Boy.

"Dead people ought to be like tires. That way you could let the air out of them and they'd be easier to carry," grumbled Tato.

"Or you could leave the air in and roll them to the grave. Course with our luck, we'd probably have a traffic accident."

Natchez opened his eyes, blinking in the harsh sunlight. He seemed surprised about something.

"I'm not dead yet," he said.

Tato shook his head. "Yes you are. Shut up!"

Natchez appealed to them. "I'm not dead. No, really, I'm almost well."

Tato and Elk Boy halted their forward progress and eyed each other uncertainly across their burden. Elk Boy shrugged. He personally could have cared less but Tato began to get angry.

"Stop making trouble. You ought to be glad we volunteered to carry you," said Tato.

Elk Boy nodded in agreement. "Some people! You lug them to hell and gone and what thanks do you get, nothing, just at the last minute, somebody wants to start an argument. That's old people for you." He shook his head, looking displeased. "You just can't do them a favor!"

Natchez tried to be reasonable. "Look, I ought to be able to tell whether I am dead or not."

Tato was furious. "Listen, old man, if we let everybody decide everything for themselves, what kind of world would this be?"

"A far better world than . . ." began Natchez but he got cut off.

"Stop your damn complaining!" admonished Elk Boy. "We are doing all the work. We are doing all the sweating. All you have to be is dead. It's easy. There's no work involved."

"Easy! Who cares about easy! Let go of me!" Natchez began to struggle in the young men's arms and it was all they could do to hold on to him. "You can't bury me! I'M NOT DEAD YET!" roared the old man.

Elk Boy almost stumbled and fell. "You opinionated old people are always making trouble. You have to have everything your way or you complain, complain, complain. Listen, at your age, you're lucky to be dead."

Natchez renewed his wriggling in their arms. It threw the young men off balance. They tripped and all three of them fell to the ground with a crash.

Natchez was the first to recover. He jumped to his feet and stood over the two fallen men.

"See. I now present an even more convincing argument. I am standing up. Could I stand up if I were dead?"

Tato dusted off the seat of his pants and helped Elk Boy to his feet. He muttered to Elk Boy, "Must be rigor mortis. I've heard of cases like this. Yep. The old man is stiff as all get out. He ain't really standing up. He's just stuck in the ground like a war lance."

"So watch this and be convinced," snapped Natchez, really almost at the end of his patience. To refute their last statement,

Natchez immediately bent over double to show his living elasticity.

The two young men stared at the old man in puzzlement. For the first time, doubt began to show on their faces. They seemed to be considering the idea that the old man might not be dead.

Natchez felt he had convinced them and tried to straighten up, but his back was locked in place.

The old man winced with pain. He tried to move but he just couldn't. He looked at the two young men with growing embarrassment. "I'm stuck! You young fellows are gonna have to help me!"

Tato and Elk Boy exchanged a knowing look.

Tato said, "He'd do anything to get out of this, wouldn't he?"

Elk Boy nodded. "Some people just don't know when to quit. They just make up any old little thing and we're supposed to buy it. Jesus! What does he think we are, a couple of tourists?"

Tato shook his head in disgust. "First he says he isn't dead, but he is; now he says he's stuck. He's a shameless old liar is what he is, if you ask me."

Elk Boy regarded the old man with disdain. "Yeah. I heard about corpses suddenly sitting up on their burial rack. Muscles spasms is what it is, or maybe they ate something that didn't agree with them and they got gas or something, you know, from stomach cramps or something like that. Well the old faker must be just having one of those damn muscle spasms. That's got to be why the old devil is now folded in two. Guy just don't know when to quit lying, is how I see it."

Natchez strained against his locked back, his face contorted with the effort.

"I TELL YOU I'M STUCK!"

Elk Boy came over, grabbed Natchez's arms from behind, put his foot on the old man's back and tried to lever him up.

The old man shrieked with pain but nothing happened.

Elk Boy said, "OK, I'll give him this one. He IS stuck! That's the most rigorous mortis I've ever seen."

Natchez looked triumphant despite his awkward position. "If I was telling the truth on this one, I could also be telling the truth about not being dead. How's that strike you?"

"Quit fooling," said Tato. "You're too dead to skin."

He bent over and stared into the old man's face. "Now you're really giving us a hard time, old man. How are we going to bury you at a right angle?"

Elk Boy nodded glumly, looking supremely unhappy. "I tell you, old people are nothing but trouble," he also bent over to look at the old man.

It looked odd with all three of them bent over in the middle of nowhere. It looked like a symbol of something or other. Nobody knew just exactly of what.

Elk Boy finally summed it up. He was disgusted. "Well, he sure isn't going to fit in the coffin that way, that's for damn sure."

Tato straightened up and moved closer to the old man. He grabbed the old man's head suddenly and tried to push it down to the ground.

"Maybe I can fold him," said Tato.

Natchez shrieked, "You maniac! I can't bend that far!"

Tato considered it, trying to think it out. "Maybe if you come over and help me, Elk Boy. We'll both jump on his head and our combined weight ought to . . ."

Natchez was so angry he rose up of his own volition, his back creaking like a skeleton falling on a tin roof.

"You got me angry now! A dead Indian is not a good Indian! My vengeful spirit is going to break your noses!" roared the old man.

"At least he admits he's dead now," said Elk Boy.

"He's a hard man to convince," said Tato.

Natchez was outraged. "I am not convinced!"

"Let's discuss it. I am willing to discuss it," said Tato.

"That's very Indian of you," observed Elk Boy.

Natchez pulled out a knife. He leaped at the two young men and stabbed Tato in the chest. Tato looked surprised and then fell down and looked dead because he was.

Natchez waved the knife in the air defiantly. "Now who's the dead one?"

Elk Boy looked at the old man, then looked down at the still body of Tato. He seemed puzzled.

"Well, I have to admit. Tato *looks* a lot more dead than you do," admitted Elk Boy.

"That's because he's dead and I'm alive."

Elk Boy shrugged. "Hard to say if he is dead or not. Maybe it was just something he ate."

Natchez pointed to the nothingness in the distance. "Why don't we pick up Tato and carry him to the burying ground?"

"It seems reasonable," said Elk Boy and they picked him up, cradling him in the same way Natchez had been carried.

They began walking across the vast empty spaces.

The dead body was heavy and it made the journey hard.

"He really looks dead," said Elk Boy. "How is it, old man, that you know who's dead and who isn't?"

"I am old and have death always on my tongue. I know the taste. Not quite as refreshing as cold beer but a taste all the same. And you . . . you are young . . . as young as I once was . . . and the young do not understand death."

Tato stirred in their arms, opening his eyes.

"I'm not dead," said Tato.

They dropped him on the ground.

The old man and the young man stood over the body of Tato. He stared up at them with the beginning of a smile on his face.

Elk Boy picked up a huge rock, lifted it over his head and then swung. It crashed down on Tato's head, killing him instantly.

The old man and the young man bent over and picked up their dead burden again. They began the long weary march to the grave.

"By the way," said Natchez, "why did you hit him with that rock?"

Elk Boy kept his face into the wind. Under his breath he muttered, "Sometimes you just get tired of life being . . . one big argument."

They had arrived at nowhere.

The Fatal Joy of Bound Woman

The white relatives were taking great care to be gentle with her because they were exceedingly tolerant.

Delicacy was the word of the hour because her heart beat weakly in her breast like a dying hummingbird and more importantly, because the news of Bound Woman's husband's death meant that they all stood to inherit a lot of money.

In the Stanhope family, a lot of money could spawn a good deal of gracious behavior.

Barrett Townsend Stanhope had been killed in a plane crash. His widow, Bound Woman, was a full-blooded Indian, Barrett's only retained eccentricity from the wild, gold-mining days that had brought all the Stanhopes wealth and position.

Bound Woman was not a well woman. Too sudden a shock might kill her, so her doctor had advised.

She sat on the daybed, dark eyes almost buried in her wrinkled face. She seemed upset by the number of people clustered around her. She hated a fuss.

Besides that, she seldom saw the other Stanhopes. They were always cordial. Her husband's money guaranteed that, but at the same time, they were never there either.

"Who died?" asked Bound Woman.

"My dear woman," said Amanda Stanhope, one of Barrett's nieces. "What makes you think somebody has died?"

"Vultures!" said Bound Woman. "That's the only time you ever come around."

Amanda paled, then her face reddened as the insult went home. So much for tact and diplomacy. She had been giving considered hints that revealed in half concealing. Apparently, the effort had been wasted on the old woman.

Doctor Maddsen held her hand. "I'm afraid it's Barrett. The

authorities have notified us that his Learjet crashed on a cliff above Morro Bay. No one could have survived the crash."

He took her pulse, fearing the worst. Bound Woman was in very frail health. Severe shock could shatter her heart.

Bound Woman's head dropped forward. Her eyes filled with tears and she wept unashamedly. Doctor Maddsen resisted the impulse to put his arm around her.

The relatives, Stanhopes young and old, had resisted that same impulse all their lives. They stood aloof from her, silently but distantly approving, waiting for the storm of grief to subside. After all, she was mourning the passing of one of their own.

Bound Woman turned her head, looking past them, looking toward the window, tears still streaking her face. She could see into the cactus garden she had planted to remind her of the land of her people so unlike this place, and it comforted her.

"It was good of you all to come," said Bound Woman.

"Nonsense," said Amanda. "You're family after all."

Bound Woman shook her head no.

"I had to pretend to be, you mean, for Barrett's sake," she said. "But I was never a member of this family."

"But of course you are," cried Amanda. Others offered like demurrers.

"Get the hell out of here!" said Bound Woman with some show of fury.

Doctor Maddsen regarded his charge with real concern.

"Perhaps it would be best if you would all go. She's had a very hard time of it. She needs to rest."

The Stanhopes turned and left, muttering under their collective breaths certain less than kind sentiments about Bound Woman. Doctor Maddsen patted her gently on her arm and also rose to go. "Try to get some sleep. I'll look in on you later before I go."

She stared out the window, giving no sign that she had even heard him.

As she stared at the garden, the beginning of a smile started on her face. Above the garden, she saw the good-tasting breath of summer rain in the sky. It wasn't the cactus garden she saw and the dead dreams she had chased in it, but Black Horse Mesa where the wind of her childhood blew, wild and strange, from a

Welcome to Lee County Main Library!

You checked out the following items:
* Death chants

Barcode: 33262000786407 Due: 09/11/2012
11:59 PM

SANFORD 2012-08-21 16:28

You were helped by Lee

Welcome to Lee County Main Library!

You checked out the following items:
* Death chants

Barcode: 33262000786407 Due: 09/11/2012
11:59 PM

SANFORD 2012-08-21 16:28

You were helped by Lee

dwelling at the center of the earth. She heard the drummers calling the young men and women out of their hogans. She heard the bone-whistle flutes and little hand-tamed birds flew in an old twilight ocean of long-ago nights.

She was like a child, toothless and wrinkled, with everything and nothing before her. It was all over now that Barrett was dead; whatever her life with him had been, it was gone.

Even as she stared at the skeletal shapes of the cacti in her garden, she sensed a change in them. As if they had lost purpose and meaning, their roots torn from the earth by a flash flood of mistaken memory. So clearly now, the garden which had always comforted her with a semblance of native land seemed alien now, the sickly flowering buds flesh white like the pulpy fingers of dead men.

Why should I feel comforted by a reminder that I am not on my native land? The garden was betrayal, an arrow of longing for a distant shore.

And she abandoned it, the cruel garden of twisted, impaling shapes, just as she now abandoned kinship with the Stanhopes, once and for all time.

Bound Woman felt something new stirring in the wind out there above the garden.

Had she tended the soil to raise green things that mocked her with death? Had she grown a desert woven out of her heart and the remembered heartland of her people, and was that all that remained of life for her to look at? No. The word was a fever, it was a move through darkness to the stars.

Dreams long forgotten caught fire and burned in the cookfire. She took the Stanhopes one by one, stacked each log of them on the fire, and warmed herself over their flaming corpses.

She remembered a child-woman dream of an obscene bird of night, a starveling, gaunt feathered shape. The obscene, blood-beaked bird that revealed the emptiness of all white men's faces, pale and white like snow in a land that has never known it.

As a child, the bird of night had been an omen and a totem that had guided her terrified child steps away from the pale-faced ones.

What terrible force had killed the dream warning of the night bird?

She had thrown her heart at strangers not born of the land, at that special one she had loved and now lost, Barrett, who silenced totems with love, murdered omens with a caress.

Truly the bird had died.

But now it seemed to be in the air once again, hovering over the upraised arms of the cacti in her garden. The growing things of her garden seemed like dead men pointing their bones at the sky. And the garden with each sharp spiny needle of knowledge, which seemed to know the coming from tale of her life, now seemed as dead as the land that held the ashes of her people.

When what she had become was undone, what was left?

Nothing and then death?

No. Something else.

Something was coming for her. Something that would at last be hers. It was a strangeness and a familiarity, unnamable, like a forbidden taste.

Still it called to her, made the blood sing in racing warmth in her tired old body, which a white man had once loved.

It was in the sky and it moved in the four sacred directions. Bound Woman held up her arms to it, but the roof overhead prevented that.

"Help!" she screamed.

There was an answering chorus, a lightning bolt of startled gasps from the other room. The room shook with a small thunder of rushed footsteps and the door to the room burst open. The Stanhopes entered en masse, with Doctor Maddsen leading an embarrassed charge up San Juan Hill.

"You must have been glued to the door," said Bound Woman with ironic glee. "Well, you can wipe the smile of hope off your face. I'm not dying, if you think that's what I was screaming about."

"My dear, I assure you," began Amanda, the apologist for the family.

"Save it," said Bound Woman. "I want to be carried outside. I want some air and some sunshine. I'm sick of this damn bed."

"I wouldn't advise—" began Doctor Maddsen.

"Then consider yourself fired," said Bound Woman.

There was an unmistakable note of command in her voice. The best Doctor Maddsen could do was see that she was not unduly jostled as several of the male Stanhopes made a chair of their arms and carried her out into the garden.

The relatives stood all around her in a half circle as she was gently lowered into a wicker lawn chair.

"Move off and give me some damn air," grumbled Bound Woman. "I came outside to see the outside, not all of you."

They moved off in a group, coming to a stop at the edge of the long circular driveway. They seemed engaged in a rather animated dispute with Doctor Maddsen. It was not a particularly happy group.

Bound Woman looked up at the sky and felt a part of herself drifting off, lured by plains of white snow to the north, long cool green rivers from the south.

She did not regret Barrett's death.

She only had one life.

She was only one person. Perhaps in this thing, which she felt in the sky, Barrett and his white ways, perhaps they had once come for her but only now did she know, that she had never really been where she had thought, and Barrett thought, she was.

She had to call to that part of herself that had always been her, before Barrett and the Stanhopes, and the kind of life made for her that had been shared and not shared in their long years together.

She touched the sky then with an Indian child's little stick hand.

The thing that approached, possessed her.

Now it was just her and the sky.

No more pretended whiteness, just whispered words that burst from her lips. "I am Indian again! I am free!"

They were words that sang in the blood. Her heart pounded with the joy of it.

Oh, there was loss, for Barrett had loved her, and she him, but they had grown into two people who were not who they once were and should always have been. She knew she would weep again when his face was in her eyes but she saw beyond that, to suddenly perceived years, that from this moment on, would belong only to her. The bird rode the sky again.

She had no one else to live for, and now under the good true sky of mother earth, could live for herself.

She could be a small child again, running to jump into the shadow of a bird flying above her.

She had lost love, a fire that warms in mystery, but gained in its loss, possession of her true self again.

She breathed a quiet prayer to the tree of all trees that life might now be long, a wish against yesterday's horrified fear that life would be all too long.

She traveled in her mind, in her sense of herself and in her freedom, and might have traveled there the rest of her days had there been no commotion.

The Stanhopes were agitated, talking loudly, making a great deal of fuss over someone who had just stepped out of a long black car.

A figure pushed through the crowd of Stanhopes. It was Barrett Stanhope, undead, unaware he had ever been thought dead.

"Bound Woman! I'm here! What's going on here?"

His voice was unmistakable, demanding, self assured, from a lifetime of being in command.

Bound Woman was pulled back by the voice, the word, free, shattering on her tongue. A bird, pierced with an arrow, screamed in the sky.

She toppled forward, dead before she hit the ground, her heart exploding into soundlessness.

Doctor Maddsen said she died of sudden shock, of a killing joy, at the unexpected return of the love she thought she had lost.

It was the truth as far as he knew it.

But something on the back of an obscene bird of night, something climbing to nothingness in the sky knew her death in another way.

She died because she had lost herself.

The Man Who Danced with Wild Horses: Novella

CHAPTER ONE

The old man sat by the burning ruin of his house. His hands still smelled of gasoline.

"I don't understand why you want to leave everything behind?" said his son, watching the old man with apprehension.

"Everything has left me behind," said Wild Horse Dancer. "My old woman is dead. My old friends are dead. And you, my son, and Makes Pretty, my only daughter, you both belong as much in the white world as I do not."

"But where will you go? What will you do?"

"The world has changed. White people now own it. I am too much of the old world to take my place among them. If I stay near this place which they say must be torn down for the big road, I would have to live with a highway through my heart. I go to the mountains to live out my last days in a place that is still my world."

"But how will you survive?"

"I won't. But I will live well as long as I can. My heart yearns for the mountains, unchanged and dark and still full of the great mystery. Yes, I go to the mountains that still look as if part of the blackness of the night lingered in them."

The old man pushed his long gray braids back over his shoulder. He turned from his burned house and stooped to pick up his rifle and his pack.

"I shouldn't let you do this," said his son. "You still have a lot of good years left."

"Left to do what? Guard the old bones of my relatives until I become old bones beside them?"

The old man stared defiantly up at the sky. "No! As I have

walked the path of life, I have learned that I am nothing, a leaf blown by the wind.

"But if my bones rest in the lap of night, even so, I would ask that you listen this last time, for a word is like a wind and a thousand words are like a storm.

"I would speak of a life lived, of what I have understood and failed to understand.

"I have a dream. My young life was wrapped in it. My old age will wear it yet again before my bones rattle on the racks of the ancestors. I would speak of a Spirit Buffalo, a demon, a human being in animal skin, a night walker! Him I must find!"

"A tale for children," said his son. "Such things never existed."

"NO!" raged the old man with sudden heat. "I saw him born. He is to be the beginning and end of my life. He is all of those things to me. I say he lives!"

"That is your quest? Your great dream?" His son's voice sprinkled a tiny rain of contempt. "You've grown old, Father. Maybe too old."

"Yes, I am old. They called me Wild Horse Dancer in my youth because I once danced with wild horses. But in the white man's world all the wild horse are now tame or dead, so perhaps now I am just Horse Dancer, living again under the sign of my first child name. That which made me a man in this world is gone. Perhaps I will be the child, Horse Dancer once again, like an old blind snake that touches its own tail and thinks wrongly that he has found a new mate."

The old man bent under the weight of his pack. He turned, shading his eyes, and stared off in the distance at the mountain.

"In my youth, the wind swept me out among the nations and tribes. I knew great battles and peace, great hunger of body and soul and feastings. I was honored and treated like a dog. I found friends among my enemies and enemies among my friends. Long I walked the stormy paths of glory and death but the Great Spirit did not destroy me.

"I have withstood much, but when my mind dwells on the Spirit Buffalo I become lost and my tongue tastes blood."

"I should stop you. The government promised you a new house. Bigger and better than the one you had. At your age, you should be content to have a nice house over your head and a warm fire where you can comfortably sit and think back on your past. Even an old dog deserves as much. There's no need for you to go. This is suicide!" said his son.

His son's beer belly ballooned over his wide belt buckle. Sweat streaked the collar of his Pendleton shirt and stained the white brim of his Stetson.

The old man began walking toward the mountain, which rose above the land like a black swan.

Wild Horse Dancer trudged on in the heat and the dust.

His son stared at him helplessly, powerless to act. When the old man went back into his own world, there was no way for the son to reach him. They lived now in worlds too unlike each other.

"Why do you want to kill yourself?" the son shouted at the old man, his words echoing like a rifle shot across the land.

Wild Horse Dancer stopped in his tracks. He turned slowly like a leaf in the wind.

He cupped his hands to his mouth and shouted back.

"Every dream is followed by awakening but the last in a man's life. And so, my son, this is the last one in mine."

CHAPTER TWO

Horse Dancer measured his ten summers against the trunk of a tree with the impatience of a boy who yearns to grow to be a man.

It was the spring of a long-ago spring, and all around the boy life stretched its many animal necks, shut its many eyes and hissed passionately toward the sunrise.

Night had been a time of fierce unrest. Wings had beat, claws had torn and rent and the quick biting snap of sex and death had sounded in the early light of dawn.

They had told him he was too young to hunt the buffalo.

And so, he stole his uncle's old one-shot rifle with the cracked wooden stock and came out on his own to show the world he was old enough to kill a buffalo.

He was old enough and good with a gun but he was not wise enough.

He passed through the trees as quiet as a trout gliding through deep water and so came unnoticed and unheard upon a mother buffalo, giving birth.

It was a wonder he was not wise enough to understand.

He did not see the great mystery unfolding. He saw only a chance to prove his manhood.

The calf was on his feet before Horse Dancer had crept within striking distance with the old rifle.

The calf wobbled on weak legs to his mother and found her milk.

Horse Dancer loaded the old gun.

The warm milk flowed slowly from mother buffalo's body into the calf's, and the first joyous strength of life began in him.

The calf, with each gulp, felt the gray confusing clouds of birth roll away until only new blue sky flickered in his eyes.

Horse Dancer steadied his gun against the wind.

The reddish-brown buffalo calf began to know time, the light and dark of it. There was a whole world to learn, if he lived. He would learn that water is silent when it is still and noisy when it runs. He would learn the wonders of night and the glories of day.

The rifle shot was bad medicine.

It wounded fatally but did not quickly kill. It was the kind of shot that makes death long and painful.

The mother buffalo cried in agony and started to walk away from her calf. She tried to run, the brave heart of the mother buffalo singing strongly to lead danger away from her calf, which she loved more than life itself, but her body was too badly broken.

She swayed a little, ran a few steps, her flanks heaving furiously.

The reddish-brown calf understood nothing of danger, only the loss of his milk and of his one big love, buffalo mother.

The little calf stumbled alongside of his mother, trying to find the rich wonderful milk of life again.

The mother buffalo couldn't run. She was too badly hurt. The little calf, confused, butted his little head against her chest, looking for the warmth of her love.

With each breath, golden red clouds swirled, falling in a red rain on the little calf.

The calf bawled, feeling the wetness all over his back from her breath. As little as he was, as new to the world, perhaps he sensed that something was terribly wrong.

Wild Horse Dancer came running through the trees, the heavy rifle catching on brush and tree limbs, slowing him down.

He burst into the clearing, feeling a great surge of triumph, of victory.

He faced the dying mother buffalo, gun proudly raised for a final, victorious killing shot, but he made a mistake.

He looked into the soft shiny eyes of mother buffalo. He saw her looking with the greatest love of all, at her little calf. Her eyes, even dying, held only love for the little calf, as if he were the only thing she could take away with her to the land of shadows.

Horse Dancer dropped the rifle, the victory gone, now ashes in his mouth.

He had killed something that loved.

A mother that loved her child.

Mother buffalo bent her head then and thrust her muzzle against the calf, gently pushing him away. Her legs gave out then and she fell on one side, like a great living tree felled by summer lightning.

The reddish-brown calf bawled, and flung himself upon the great shuddering heap of flesh and bones that was becoming nothing.

And the little calf raised his muzzle from the body of his dead mother, his eyes staring at the new blue sky and he wailed.

Later, the rifle forgotten and lost in the place where it was dropped, for which later there would be punishment, in a night that could not begin to wash away the remembered horror of the day, the boy found comfort in his mother's arms.

The crime had been explained and understood and even forgiven, but Horse Dancer was like a bird stopped suddenly in flight.

As he lay in the dark beside the sleeping form of his mother, he thought he heard something.

He started, lifting his head, his crow-black hair shining in a beam of moonlight.

There, he heard it again.

From somewhere in the dark forest where the mountain began, an eerie animal cry reached his ears.

It was not wolf or elk. It was more like the mourning cry of a dying human being.

The horror of the day raced up the boy's spine. It couldn't be. His ears strained to hear the sound again, his body rigid.

But he heard nothing for a long time except the usual sounds of night.

The lodge was warm. Sleep began to call him again.

The wind, yes, it must have been the wind, and with that comforting thought Horse Dancer settled into the delicious sleep of a held child.

And for a while, the boy's sleep was deep and undisturbed. But then the sounds came again, louder and closer.

And the boy was thrown into wakefulness like a sleeping cat splashed with icy water. He gently threw off the comforting arm of his mother and crept silently out the door of the lodge.

Somewhere up on the mountain, the mournful wails came keening down toward the boy.

"I'm sorry," whispered the boy.

He knew it must be the buffalo calf whose mother he had killed. Now the slowly starving little animal stumbled through the night searching the world for a mother that was no longer in it.

As the boy stood there, the cry of the little calf grew louder and closer.

It sounded like it was running toward him.

Horse Dancer stared straight ahead, tring to make out the figure of the little buffalo calf in the bright moonlight.

The sound got closer. Now it was coming almost from where the boy stood, but there was nothing there.

Ice touched the boy's spine.

Now the wailing, piteous cry of the buffalo calf came from the ground where the terrified boy stood, but no buffalo calf was there.

And then the sound came from directly above him, high in the sky, and stayed up there, and passed beyond him, like a flock of geese journeying into winter, and then softly, grew faint and disappeared in the distance.

Then the boy looked up at the sky in both wonder and terror in equal measure.

Surely Horse Dancer had heard the cry of a Spirit Buffalo and it would have some great meaning to him around which he could build his life.

Perhaps the Spirit Buffalo knew how sorry he was and had forgiven him.

He only knew, in his folly, he had tasted manhood and the beginning of its sorrow.

Now, he stared at the sky, and wondered in his rapidly beating heart, if he had also, touched magic.

CHAPTER THREE

The magic did not go away.

The Spirit Buffalo, in forms and faces of its own choosing, continued to touch his life as he lived it.

In Horse Dancer's seventeenth summer he met a man born with the dead.

For three moons the man born with the dead wandered the hills and valleys with a sharp digging stick, searching for the lost grave of his long dead wife.

Horse Dancer's people did not look in the man's eyes when he walked by. They said the shadow of the grave was in them, and was not good to look upon.

They called him Looks For Death.

Another man had taken his wife in the dead of a long-ago winter. They had fled into the mountains to escape the wrath of her husband. A blizzard had overtaken them and neither of them had ever been seen again.

Somewhere on the mountain, their bones lay entwined where deadly winter overtook them, buried treasure for the man who sought it. That they had met their deaths and slept on the mountain together, that was commonly known, for a traveler had found them and buried them on the spot where they had died. The traveler told everyone he met of the tragedy but his directions were not clear and no one had ever found their lonely grave.

It was whispered ever so softly, so softly that not even the spirits of the wind dancing outside the lodges, could hear it, that Looks For Death's wife had stolen away some great treasure, a medicine bundle given to man by the Great Thunderbird.

Whether Looks For Death sought treasure or bones, none could say for sure, but the mountain was scarred from end to end by the marks of his digging stick.

Horse Dancer saw him many times that first summer.

Always from a distance at first, but later Looks For Death began coming down closer and closer to the village.

Close up, it was easy to see Looks For Death was starving. His ribs were showing, his eyes bright, glazed and sunken in his face. His legs dragged like they were turning into heavy logs.

Horse Dancer took food to him.

The old man stared at Horse Dancer. He made no move to touch the food.

Then suddenly he leaped forward and tore the meat and corncakes out of the boy's hand. He was like a wolf stealing bait from a snare.

He gulped the food down ravenously.

Looks For Death changed before the startled boy's eyes. The old man became strong, his back straightened, and he seemed full of life once more.

He ran to a hill, thrust his digging stick into the hard ground. He scraped furiously at the hard earth.

Horse Dancer just stood there, watching the strange old man.

Looks For Death stepped into the hole he had gouged out. He turned and looked back at the boy.

The look of madness in his eyes swirled like a cloud blown by the wind.

"This old buffalo man gives thanks for what has been given!" The old man's voice was like a cold wind.

The boy nodded once and turned to go.

"I have danced in all the houses of death!" shrieked Looks For Death, and his eyes rolled in his head. "I am a fly on the sweet honey of death!"

Horse Dancer knew then that the old man was mad.

"I cry for her, she who I have lost. She was every day of my life and her going left me forever in the night."

Horse Dancer also knew that the old man's madness came from grief and sorrow and loss, and his fear of the strange man was lessened in the knowing.

Looks For Death fell to his knees, his arm wrapped around the length of his digging stick, as if he hugged a woman.

"I love her," he said simply, his voice breaking and he wept unashamedly.

Then, as the boy stood beside the fallen figure of the old man, he knew for the first time a sense of some of the deepness of the human heart in this world.

Horse Dancer ran away.

He had seen too much.

Later, to deny what the young must always try to deny, he joined in a trick played upon the old man.

In the dark, he and two other boys his own birth age crept up on the old man and tossed some animal bones into a hole he was digging.

When he found them, at sunrise, Looks For Death was delirious with joy and grief and clasped them lovingly to his breast.

When he knew, after a time, that they were not human bones, his terrible grief made Horse Dancer and his friends sick at heart.

It was a trick they wished never to have done.

Then one day, a bright, chilly day with the first icy breath of winter in it, Looks For Death disappeared.

He was gone all that winter, where, no one knew.

Most thought he was dead.

But the first days of summer brought Looks For Death back to the mountain.

One night Horse Dancer saw him moving in the mountains, like an old gray bird with wings outstretched. Horse Dancer gathered up some food, and hurried down to meet him, the memory of his unkind trick still strong and stinging in his mind.

Somewhere in the dark he lost sight of him.

Toward morning, he spied a light coming from a stand of pine trees and he went to investigate.

He heard a sound then, the loud rasp of a digging stick thudding into the slowly thawing ground, and he knew it was Looks For Death.

A moment later he saw him.

The old man was bent to the earth, digging.

Horse Dancer thought of an old bear digging its winter cave. He had seen a bear dig just like this as it prepared for its journey into sleep.

Horse Dancer thought then that he must speak to Looks For Death. Even though everybody in the village was afraid of him.

"I brought you some food."

Horse Dancer held out a quickly wrapped bundle of food.

"Soon," said the old man. "I know her bones are near."

Horse Dancer set the parcel of food at Looks For Death's feet. The old man stared at it blankly. Then he looked up into the face of the young boy. He smiled.

"I knew you would come. You were sent to hear my tale, to see my last triumph! For you see, I have found that which I seek."

Horse Dancer did not know what to make of that. He just stood there quietly, waiting to see what the strange old one would do.

Looks For Death pointed to the western slope of the mountain.

"I sat on the highest ledge, letting the sun burn the last taste of winter out of my blood when I saw lightning moving along the mountainside. No clouds were in the sky but the lightning walked on the ground until it came to this hill where I now stand. Then it flashed up toward the sky and bathed this mound in the lightning flash of a thousand thousand summer storms. Then it was gone, back into the sky, but this hill glowed like the coals of a fire."

The old man touched his chest above his heart with his hand. "Then in my heart, I knew that this was an omen, a great sign that had been sent to me."

Horse Dancer stood there awkwardly, not sure how to feel about this strange tale.

"When I came down to this place where I now dig, a great unseen hand seemed to pull my digging stick, until it twisted like a living snake in my hands, pointing to this place like a great finger."

Horse Dancer saw that there was a small burial mound built by human hands. The ground was hard-packed yellow clay with large flat stones piled up around it. It seemed to fit the traveler's description of the grave the traveler said he had made long ago for Looks For Death's wife and her lover.

"You must eat," said Horse Dancer. "Eat to regain your strength and I will help you dig."

"Yes," he agreed. "I will build a fire while you dig."

The old man sat down beside the packet of food.

Looks For Death seemed on the verge of total exhaustion.

Horse Dancer built the fire himself because the old man did not move at all now. He just sat there, looking dazed.

The warmth of the fire seemed to revive the old man. He took the food finally and gulped it down like a starving bear after a winter's fast.

"Soon the bones will shine in the light of day," he said, watching as Horse Dancer began to dig.

The boy dug silently, keeping his eyes on the old man, not looking at him directly but keeping him in sight nevertheless. Looks For Death seemed like a shadow himself, like a being from some forgotten grave. Even his clothes seemed to reek of the grave. The old man was dressed in old buckskin, cracked and stiff with dirt.

"I will never leave this mountain," said Looks For Death. "When I have found the bones, I will build my lodge here and will sit among them and gaze upon the great mystery stretched out before me."

The sharpened end of the digging stick raked the ground.

Looks For Death smiled then, and his eyes stared at something far away. His eyes dulled, touched some sorrow and became troubled. "But when death overtakes me with the long-sought bones, I will come back to this place in the shape of a great spirit creature! Then you shall meet me again. I will come back to this place in the shape of a great spirit creature!"

Looks For Death started, his ears straining to hear something Horse Dancer could not hear. The old man rose to his feet, his face contorted, shadows thrown across it by the fire. A strangeness possessed him.

He stepped forward, tried to raise his arms up to the sky. He fell forward, his face almost in the fire.

Horse Dancer flung the digging stick aside, leaping out of the hole.

The old man was in the grip of some madness, his eyes rolled up, his legs pulled up under his body like leaves shriveling in a fire.

A savage groan escaped from the depths of Looks For Death's throat. His body arched spasmodically on the ground like a snake with a broken back.

Horse Dancer dragged him away from the fire.

The body thrashed, writhed and then, slowly, relaxed and twitched no more, like a body tired to death.

Horse Dancer bent over the body and noticed that the sound of Looks For Death's breathing was growing weaker. He had to bend over close to the body to even sense it.

He put his hand on the old one's chest and felt the last few heartbeats dance in Looks For Death's body and then they were gone, as Looks For Death was gone.

The old man lay dead across the final triumph of his life. For the last stroke of the digging stick had turned over the bones of she, Looks For Death had so long sought.

Now the old man was dead on a hill of the dead. Only Horse Dancer and the fire burned with life beside him.

What were the last words the old man spoke?

Horse Dancer buried Looks For Death with the lost and now found bones of his wife. He wished to leave everything he knew of the strange old man, here on the burial mound, in the kind, hiding earth that knows how to forget.

But after that night, Horse Dancer had to carry within him the last words of Looks For Death.

"I will come back in the shape of a great spirit creature."

When night spread her robe of sleep over the sky, Horse Dancer saw spirit creatures moving like hungry shadows in the forest. It was then he heard the words again.

"In the shape of a great spirit creature."

And however much he tried to still the sound of it, it made his heart beat like the crash of animals meeting in secret combat.

When night fled, and dawn eased the tyranny of what lives in the dark, Horse Dancer listened for other voices: The courtship songs of birds, the whisper of the trees as they talked to the wind. He heard these voices that had been his to hear since the first days he walked the earth. These were the wordless languages of the world but yet he thought he heard another voice, far away.

It made him think of the Sky People the old people talked about, even though it was not something in which his heart strongly believed.

But with the passing of Looks For Death, the words of wind in the forest seemed to whisper, "Spirit Creature."

In the next years of his life, Horse Dancer was in constant dread of something he sensed must happen.

The waiting for it was like a knife blade scraped across the edge of his soul.

Now night and the forest became a fascination for him.

Horse Dancer had never known fear in his world of mountain and forest, not even when the animals he hunted turned on him at the end of the chase, murderous black bear with death in one swipe of its great claws, wolf, mountain lion, all deadly in their own way.

If it was not fear, it was a sense of strangeness that overtook Horse Dancer. It seemed to spring equally from the last promise of Looks For Death and Horse Dancer's memory of the magic of a Spirit Buffalo, long ago.

Now when Horse Dancer killed an animal, he looked first into its eyes.

Why and for what did he look?

Horse Dancer knew.

Once, long ago, so the story went among his people, Kahtanis, the greatest of the chiefs of old, had a daughter as good to look upon as the soft honey moon. But like a honey moon, the black bear of disease gobbled her up, and though she tried to stay in the sky in her boy husband's arms, the black bear was too strong for her.

As she fell from the sky, she promised to come back to he whom she loved in the shape of a bird.

She died and the earth grew over her bones.

That next summer, a partridge appeared on the still-grieving husband's house. At first the bird was shy and vanished in full flight when spoken to but the female bird came back again and again. And she came back only to him.

Soon the bird was eating out of the young man's hands.

When winter came the partridge changed her feathers, became snowy white and flew straight up toward the sun, never to be seen again.

The girl had kept her word.

How could Horse Dancer not expect Looks For Death to keep his?

It happened that next spring.

Horse Dancer was hunting on the western slopes of the mountain, not far from where the bones of Looks For Death were buried. It was late in the day.

The snow, was still hard enough to bear his weight. He moved silently through a world still white with winter's last gift.

The sun flamed red in the sky, promising the end of winter. Water, as cold as the snow it had just been, cascaded down the mountain.

He was walking bent over, his eyes intent on the tracks of a deer that had passed before him.

Then he heard the scream of a crow above him.

He raised his face to the sky.

When a crow screamed like that, some evil was loose in the world.

Horse Dancer saw bad medicine in many things, but the scream of a crow augured the worst.

He remembered one other time when he had heard a crow scream. He had been hunting on the north slope of the mountain when crystal clear, he had heard a crow scream as it flew up out of a stand of young pine trees.

Horse Dancer followed it into the trees.

There he found the skeleton of a man hanging from the trees. How it got there he could not guess and did not want to know.

Horse Dancer fled and the crow flew over him, screaming, as if mocking him.

So it was that Horse Dancer was convinced that the crow, the eater of the dead, was an ill omen.

Horse Dancer marked the flight of the crow. The black eater

of the dead was sure to have seen something strange down there in the forest.

"Raaaaaaaaateee Taaaateee!" cried the crow.

Horse Dancer moved west, away from the crow, deeper into the fall of night. He had not slept for two days and would gladly have stayed awake another night and all the coming nights of the world, for he loved night, but dawn was approaching.

A wintry, cold dawn and with it, a growing sleepiness.

He intended to climb only one more ridge, then find shelter and sleep, but as he reached the top of the ridge above Spirit Lake, something happened that murdered all thought of sleep.

In the mist, in the first burst of sun through the trees, he saw a great dark buffalo cow standing over a newborn white buffalo calf.

No such calf had even been born on this world before. Only a few minutes old, steamy with the warmth of the afterbirth, it stood calmly in the snow as its mother licked its wet white coat.

Horse Dancer had never heard of a buffalo calf being born in winter. Spring was only beginning. Here in the mountains, winter still held the world in its icy grip. There was a season for birth but this was not its time. Such a thing could not happen but it had.

This white buffalo calf then was a spirit being, white as the winter spirit that must be its buffalo father.

Horse Dancer stood there, unable to move, drawn to the sight, yet wanting to flee because this was a thing beyond his understanding.

The wind changed direction and Horse Dancer's smell reached the buffalo cow. Her head came up and she regarded him without fear.

Horse Dancer shivered in the presence of mystery.

The mother buffalo turned and fled, not in alarm, not in fear, but as if there were some reason for her to be gone.

The newborn calf spun around on wobbly legs, looking in the boy's direction. The white calf bellowed at him and Horse Dancer found himself walking toward the little white one.

He came quite close and the calf did not run. He bent down to the animal. It seemed to move toward his embrace, the warm coat steaming in the cool dawn.

The white one looked up into Horse Dancer's eyes and that great knife waiting in his soul, moved and turned and went inward. And he knelt there like a healer in prayer.

The white buffalo's eyes were not the soulless eyes of the newborn. They were old human eyes. Full of pain and wonder and remembrance.

Above Horse Dancer, the crow circled round and round, screaming, until suddenly the black one darted to the west and its ominous cry died away.

As Horse Dancer hugged the white calf to him, he felt its brave heart beating and he saw that it was a bull calf.

He felt a sudden need to look up at the sky and as he did, he had a vision. He saw Looks For Death again standing on the bones of his loved one. And he saw the great snake of his own life unfold itself, and as it went by in the darkness he saw the scar made in his snake skin by the passing of Looks For Death.

As he had been marked in life, so too must he mark the Spirit Buffalo's life so that there would be one great shared life between them.

He took out his hunting knife and laid the blade against the right ear of the white buffalo calf.

Gently, asking the buffalo's spirit for forgiveness, he cut the ear of the buffalo calf.

Then he threw the knife away.

He stood up and the spirit calf bawled for its mother.

Horse Dancer went away and did not look back.

He just ran back up the ridge, not alarmed, not in fear, but as if he, too, now had a reason to be gone.

CHAPTER FOUR

Wild Horse Dancer surprised himself by surviving the first winter.

He had been afraid his old bones would not carry him through the whole winter, but they had found new, unknown strength. Perhaps it was the wind of the mountain at his back, driving him on into another year.

Already spring was touching the wind. He lay awake in the

warmth of the lodge he had built for himself. He lived now in his memories and in dreams of a white buffalo calf.

A dream seemed to come to him again and again. He lay awake remembering it.

It was always the same dream, it always happened the same way.

White men were on the mountain, hunting buffalo. It seemed to be happening a long time ago when Wild Horse Dancer was young and Wild was not yet added to his name.

A tall man led them, long rifle glinting in the sun. They had killed many buffalo, more than any tribe could eat in a season, and yet they still hunted.

A great buffalo cow, hiding its half-grown calf with its own body, broke from cover in front of them.

The long rifle came up, spoke once and the great buffalo cow fell to the ground, dead with one shot.

As the mother cow fell, only then did Horse Dancer see the calf clearly.

It was snow white with a slit in its right ear.

It was the winter spirit calf with human eyes.

Shots rang out, but the white calf ran into the trees, eluding them.

Horse Dancer ran after the winter spirit calf. He heard it cry out like a human in pain, a sound echoing through the mountain like no sound ever uttered by an animal before.

Horse Dancer ran and ran but he could not catch up to the Spirit Buffalo. He knew it was a Spirit Buffalo because the tracks of it were like no buffalo tracks he had ever seen.

He knew he would be able to tell those tracks from a thousand. They were larger than they should be, slightly pointed at the front of the print, as if a spear point had been pressed to the ground at the start of each footprint.

The fire in Horse Dancer's lodge slowly went out with tiny cracking sounds but his mind was on the dream and he was unaware.

Outside the lodge a hungry fox stopped to smell the fire smoke lingering in the air.

Somewhere up the mountain, in this dream of long ago, the white men laid down their guns and slept beside Spirit Lake, whose waters were restless at night with the near presence of the strange white men. Only Horse Dancer, hiding in the trees beside their camp, was awake.

He was the only witness.

Beside the troubled water of Spirit Lake, a half-grown white buffalo calf licked the dark brown skin of its mother, which hung on a pole fastened to two trees.

The calf kept caressing it with his muzzle but no life called to his life. The skin was no longer his warm, loving mother.

The young buffalo, with the tortured eyes of Looks For Death, raised to the sky and cried hoarsely and brokenly.

The lodge was as quiet as a good woman's grave. The cold grew bold at the death of the fire, and began to fill the lodge. But in that silence slowly grew the voices, ever present, that had walked with Horse Dancer most of his days.

Looks For Death's voice. The Spirit Buffalo's voice. These voices sounded as one.

It was as if spirits were singing to him in the wind and the song was of the dead coming back, of the dead coming back, as Great Spirit Creatures.

CHAPTER FIVE

Sometimes Wild Horse Dancer traveled down the mountainside, toward the places where other people lived.

On the lower slopes, Indians and some whites lived a precarious existence, wresting what living they could from the mountain's bounty.

Their houses were clustered together. The people who lived there dreamed of quiet death, seemed only to be waiting for the mountain to call them back to earth.

Wild Horse Dancer's lodge was on the windy top of a ridge, jutting out over a river. If the snows of winter were too heavy, the floods of spring would wash it away.

Sky Speaker, an old shaman, lived on the lower slopes. He was one of Wild Horse Dancer's few friends among the people who lived on the lower reaches of the mountain. He was a man born old and now he was deeper into the long-seeing night of mystery. His whole life had been visions. Women, love, children, the things that tie a man to earth, these had been as nothing to him.

Sky Speaker had felt himself drawn to the old man because of Wild Horse Dancer's strange ways and even stranger dreams.

Wild Horse Dancer slept during the day and roamed and prowled the night, like a nocturnal hunting beast.

When his kinsmen shut their lodges tight against the chill winds of night, and let their fires burn low, Wild Horse Dancer's fire was just beginning.

Before the moon climbed its highest in the sky, Wild Horse Dancer escaped into the woods, only to return to his lodge at dawn. Then he would creep in, curl up like an animal in its den and sleep.

Sky Speaker could see the wind and hear time and swallow day and night and he was always called to sing the evil spirits out of the newly dead at funerals. And so it was to him, that the people turned for an explanation of Wild Horse Dancer's strangeness.

"There are two kinds of human beings," Sky Speaker said. "Those born by day and those born by night. Those born by night have a strange longing for darkness. Such a being is Wild Horse Dancer."

The old shaman was right about Wild Horse Dancer.

To Wild Horse Dancer in the last days of life, the sunshine was not warm but cold, while the moon was quite different.

In the light of the burning moon, the forest shadows were the dancing, leaping spirits of dead animals, immense, spinning, smoke-colored shapes, almost invisible and yet unmistakable. Then, as he moved among them, Wild Horse Dancer felt as if he were some great stalking fire-warmed god of death himself.

It was only then that he felt alive.

Watched by unseen eyes from the dark forest, where clawed feet ran, hungry-formed beasts of prey crouched, the whole forest felt like the very center of the one great mystery.

There was a voice in the air, always speaking to him, and at times he even felt he could hear the stars burning in the sky.

And somewhere, out there in that place of gathering mystery, the Spirit Buffalo waited for him. Someday he would find it, when the signs were favorable and his time had come.

Wild Horse Dancer was not to spend the rest of his days alone.

A blind, eyeless hawk found its way to his door one dark and stormy night. It had been struck down by something, its face was claw-marked, two empty eye sockets glaring out.

By all rights, it should have been dead, but it seemed to defy death's sting.

Wild Horse Dancer did not know what to make of this sullen feathered stranger rasping at the door of his lodge. Kill it and put it out of its misery, that was his first thought, for wounded as it was, it could not survive.

But the more Wild Horse Dancer watched how the hawk handled itself—not fearing him as the old man picked it up and carried it inside, just waiting patiently in his hands until he set it gently on the floor—the more he became convinced that the bird had some special reason for being there.

Perhaps this bird was a messenger.

Wild Horse Dancer cut a small slab of deer meat and put it on the dirt floor of the lodge. The hawk attacked the meat immediately, falling upon it ravenously.

Wild Horse Dancer was not so sure that he had not been visited by some spirit.

Not knowing what else to do, he sewed a small hood, made of a spare piece of buckskin, and fitted it to the hawk's head, so that the gaping eye sockets would not be exposed to the air.

The bird bore the donning of the hood with good grace.

The meat gone, the bird walked slowly to one corner of Wild Horse Dancer's lodge. It scratched the dirt floor as if checking the firmness of the ground. It squawked once; what that meant, Wild Horse Dancer did not know. Then it put its head under one wing and went to sleep.

Wild Horse Dancer sat in the firelight, staring with mingled wonder and fear at his visitor. The bird seemed to have made this its home, for whatever reason. Wisely, Wild Horse Dancer sensed that what had happened had no explanation a mere human being could understand.

He called the hawk by no name. If it was a spirit, it would already have a name of its own and would need no name of Wild Horse Dancer's choosing.

The next day, the bird was still there and hungry. The old man fed him more meat, which seemed to suit the bird very well.

The old man had gathered his gear to go hunting late one night. With a squawk, the bird hopped toward him as he started to go out the door of the lodge. Wild Horse Dancer turned to see what was disturbing the bird. The bird flapped its wings, gained the air and landed heavily on his shoulder.

The old man winced as the bird's claws found purchase on his shoulder.

"You are a strange one, bird," said the old man. "Perhaps you lived once with men before. Perhaps your secret heart name is known to another man who once walked this earth? Or are you just a spirit, come to me for I know not what reason?"

The bird said nothing in reply.

Wild Horse Dancer tried to take the bird off his shoulder, but the hawk screeched and stabbed at the old man with his beak, trying to bite him.

Wild Horse Dancer let him stay there. The bird rode quietly on his shoulder all through the long night of hunting. It was a strange thing to see, an old man traveling the mountain at night with a blind hawk on his shoulder.

Strange it seemed to Wild Horse Dancer himself, but there was a rightness about the hawk sitting there on his shoulder, just a feeling that Wild Horse Dancer felt washing over him, but it made him oddly content.

So together, they searched the night for a great spirit creature.

As they traveled, in the houses of those they did not visit, beside the social fires of white and Indian alike, the legend of the beast, the White Spirit Buffalo, that Wild Horse Dancer and the hawk sought was told and retold, until, like a dark seed planted in the minds of men, it grew.

Unknown to Wild Horse Dancer, a tale was being told about a great white buffalo, a spirit being, that no bullet could touch, half body and half spirit, that no hunter could conquer.

CHAPTER SIX

A year passed. Wild Horse Dancer still walked the nights on the mountain and so, too, walked the White Spirit Buffalo.

The people on the mountain called the great buffalo, Sky Moon. Why they called him that, no one could say. Such names float on the winds of winter and have no source known to man.

Sky Moon wandered the mountain like a being half of body and half of spirit. Hunters coming upon him suddenly could not seem to get off a shot at him, or if they did, the bullets just could not reach him.

During the mating season, the world of the mountain shook at dawn at Sky Moon's mating call. It was a cry from the ancient heart of the old ones, this mating challenge that thundered from his throat.

Men on the mountain who heard it, were never quite the same afterward, or so it was said.

But Sky Moon was only rarely seen, and then only as a blinding flash of white. His tracks they found aplenty, but few of those who lived on the mountain could claim to have actually seen him.

There was from time to time a determined hunter who tried to chase down Sky Moon, but the tracks seemed to stretch into infinity itself and no hunter lasted more than three days on the Night Creature's track.

But there was one man who tracked him tirelessly, day in and day out. An old man with an eyeless hawk on his shoulder.

Once, as dawn was beginning to break on the tops of the mountain, Wild Horse Dancer thought he saw the great Spirit Buffalo, just for the briefest instant, but when he had run to the spot where he sighted him, there was no trace, none.

And even the tracks had disappeared.

To chase a spirit is to chase a shadow. And so it was, that the first year passed.

CHAPTER SEVEN

The wind howled down from the black secret heart of the North. Great trees bent in the fury of the wind. On a ridge, immovable, stood Sky Moon, defiantly facing into the wind.

It was the time of day when wild animals, unable to withstand wind's fury, go softly to their hidden lairs, crouch down in fear and close their eyes and wait for the Thunder Shaker to pass away from them.

In the storm, all creatures become one, finding in the icy embrace of wind and night the tiniest of respites in their endless battles of death and life, of those who cry to be fed and those fed upon.

Here and there, blood stained the snow like a moist red flower, where a combat had been won or lost, but now was forgotten in the newer, more dangerous battle of a great storm.

The wind rose in fury but still Sky Moon did not move. His wild fierce head stood out clearly against the sky. His eyes were like stars gleaming in silvered paleness.

No animal born of other animals, could face the wind like that. Great trees from the days of the Ancients that stood like silent Gods on the ridge, loosened at their roots, leaned and bent and began to fall, destroyed in the thunderous wintry blast of the North.

Sky Moon raised his head and, full-throated, issued his challenge to the world. It drove into the face of the wind, met it and conquered it, and the wind died and was no more.

Wild Horse Dancer, stirring in his sleep, heard Sky Moon's cry and bolted upright. The voice seemed to be calling him.

He shook off the blankets as easily as he had shaken off sleep. The eyeless hawk found his shoulder somehow in the darkness of the lodge.

The wind seemed to howl like a singed wildcat outside the lodge. The frail dwelling rocked and shook in the wind, threatening to take flight.

Wild Horse Dancer threw his heaviest blanket over his shoulders and stumbled outside the lodge to face the wind. But at the moment he had stepped outside, the wind died, not subsiding, just simply ceasing to be.

Wild Horse Dancer stared at the ridge above his lodge.

Sky Moon was there, a spirit as old and as pale white as death in the snow.

Off in the distance, a night being, some great dark bird, cawed once and then fell silent again, like a life that dies just as it is born.

The great beast's head turned slowly and its eyes, burning

with strange life, seemed to pierce Wild Horse Dancer, striking deeply to the bone.

Wild Horse Dancer started moving toward the Spirit Buffalo but with the first step the earth shook and opened at his feet. He slid on the ice and went tumbling forward into an abyss.

He struck his head on something. He must have, because a blackness descended on him, and a cold, unnatural sleep possessed him.

His eyes opened but they were not his eyes. Now he saw the world through the eyes of Sky Moon. His being was wrapped in the Spirit Buffalo's skin and he let himself be part of it.

In his youth, through much suffering and pain, he had sought vision to gain power and strength. Now old, he knew himself in the presence of a greater thing, a vision that now sought him.

Wild Horse Dancer felt the cold air of morning running through his nose. His eyes burned, not from the stinging bite of the cold wind but from the eternal rhythm.

The call of mating that blazed within him.

Wild Horse Dancer pawed the ground with his mighty hooves and sniffed the wind and listened.

He smelled the end of winter in the wind of a dying storm, a green smell of earth returning.

But no scent of female buffalo danced on the wind.

Still, he sought them on the wind. Drawing air into his huge shaggy chest, he opened his mouth and sounded the mating call.

The thunder of it crashed and echoed across the mountainside.

His ears pricked up, alert for an answering call that did not come.

Wild Horse Dancer bellowed and then charged down the mountain slope, covering the ground at great speed, cleft hooves slashing against the thawing ground like lightning bolts.

He was Wild Horse Dancer and he was not. His blood and Sky Moon's were one, head and heart joined in this strange vision.

A strange scent came to them, man inside spirit animal. An ancient smell that made the blood race and the heart thunder in their mighty chest.

Sky Moon topped a small hill, and stood in a stand of small

pine trees where the smell was strongest. He swung his head, seeking the source of the scent.

Something moved, something brown stirred in the underbrush. Sky Moon was alert, eyes wide, muscles taut. A soft-skinned, sloe-eyed buffalo cow moved toward him through the trees.

She stopped moving and both animals stood there for a moment, heads stiff, eyeing each other cautiously.

Wild Horse Dancer felt a great upwelling in the strong heart of Sky Moon. A great fire burned.

This was not a buffalo cow like others of its kind. It had been touched or shaped by spirits. A great dark mark on the buffalo's back stained its coat where some great ages-old creature had left its mark on it.

The mark was in the shape of a splayed hoof, perfectly formed, not twisted and bent like a demon's.

Sky Moon strutted forward, circling the cow carefully.

She was the offspring of the Ancient of Buffalos, proud daughter of First Mother of All. She lowered her head, accepting his proprietory motions with patient, expectant grace.

A fire burned also in her.

Then, in one great rush, Sky Moon was upon her. Wild Horse Dancer lived the ancient wild dance that Sky Moon and his mate danced. It was a strange wine that sang strongly in the blood.

Wild Horse Dancer felt as light as light. He danced upward, in exultation, and his mighty hooves kicked the blue out of the sky.

And then all was quiet. Peace spread across the hill and seemed to drown the slowly greening world around them.

But the peace did not last.

The pine trees shook with the passing of another.

Something moved down through the trees toward Sky Moon and the buffalo cow.

Something evil from another world.

And the evil from another world had guns and bullets and eager white eyes and hands. It had a heart of steel that could never understand the brave heart of a Great Spirit Buffalo.

And most terrifying of all, it had a desire for a white buffalo robe. And a lust for a head that it did not know was sacred, a need to possess Sky Moon's silvery head, to butcher it and preserve it from earth's loving decay and hang it on a wall, to prove a white man's cold skill with a gun.

And from that time on, Wild Horse Dancer found something he had lost.

He could not have put a name to it, but perhaps it was a reason to live. Something worth fighting for and against.

He was Wild Horse Dancer and he was not. He was that and something else. Something more than himself. He and the White Spirit Buffalo now shared the same wild heart.

And as a group of white hunters moved into the mountain to stalk the sacred white buffalo, so did Wild Horse Dancer come at them, like a vengeful ghost under a stalking moon.

The lines of battle were clearly drawn.

They had high-powered rifles with long-vision hunting scopes, hunting dogs and enough men to beat the slopes. They were good at hunting, seasoned and methodical and inescapable.

Wild Horse Dancer was old, with only an eyeless hawk as an ally and a shared buffalo-heart dream.

Ten white men went into the mountains to kill a sacred buffalo.

One old man went into the mountains to find his name. To be in a world where the child Horse Dancer had moved toward light, had danced with untamed horses in the sanctity of youth and now age. And now once again, he rode the path of his own manhood and he was Wild Horse Dancer again, not an old man, weak with age, but a comet with fiery intent and a reason to live or to die.

What happened to those white men, who went to kill Sky Moon, the great buffalo with the eyes of Looks For Death, nobody knows.

If somebody knows, nobody is telling. None of the people who live on the lower slopes of the mountains have ever even talked about it, at least not to the strangers who came to look for the lost white men.

Those white men who went up the mountain, never came back down.

A shaman who knew an old man who walked the mountain night after night, searching for a Spirit Buffalo, said those white men froze to death and that someday their bodies would be found, when the snow melts.

Maybe that's true.

But sometimes, when the wild mountain wind howls outside their cabins and men move closer to the fire to keep the warmth from melting from their bones, a whisper begins, and there is, in very quiet, hushed voices, a tale told of an old man and a White Buffalo Spirit.

If you have never heard the tale, it goes something like this.

They say that on stormy nights near the top of the mountain, the sound of gunfire seems to come from the center of the wind. And that anyone brave enough to travel in the direction the wind comes, a man bold enough to drive on into the face of the storm, can see something he'll remember for all the days of his life.

They say a group of men is up there on the mountain, on a stony ledge, right in the path of the fiercest wind. And they are all crouched down there, with guns at their shoulder, firing at something off in the distance.

They say you can see it as plain as day.

And then the thing in the distance seems to come closer. There is a sound like the earth splitting in half and all the demons of sky and air, are screaming and then the men rise up in terror and try to run.

But the thing that had been far away, is upon them now, and where they are on the ledge, there is just no place to run to.

And then they swear this is what happens next.

The bullet-riddled corpse of an old man, with an eyeless hawk on his shoulder, sits astraddle a snow-white buffalo with eyes of fire and ice.

The hawk screams like something from the thirteenth hell, and dead man, blind hawk and white buffalo, like three dark things of the storm, thunder together across the ledge and trample the men to death.

And they say the red blood flows like a river and spills the life of everyone in its path down the side of the mountain like an evil rain.

And the sound is terrible, of hooves striking flesh, tearing and rending, and life sickening, as it destroys the courage of the listener with the final futile thud of bullets driving home in the Sacred White Buffalo's flesh.

And they say death takes them all, bird, sacred buffalo, dead man and trampled men.

And they vanish. Perhaps to the place where storms come from.

But they always return, when the storms on the mountain are at their worst.

It is a horror that few men want to see. So the tale is not told often.

But if you've heard it, perhaps they've told you the thing that scares people most.

When the blood flows thickest, and the men are twisted with death and screaming, and the White Buffalo staggers with the mortal weight of the bullets in its body, when the eyeless head of the bird is blown off by a bullet and the chest of the dead man astride the White Buffalo, has been torn away by shot and shell, then when death has touched everyone, they say, the corpse on the buffalo's back, turns his head and looks in the direction of anyone there to see it.

And then he smiles as if he knew a secret.

And the real horror would be, that you might understand it.